How I Spent My Summer Vacation

Elizabeth Fields

6-16-12

ISBN: 0615643493
ISBN-13: 978-0615643496

DEDICATION

My mom and dad, Janet and Edmond Fields, thank you for everything. I wouldn't be where I am today without your love and support. I love you. Thanks for always believing in me and for telling me so.

Doniece and everyone at Mother Hubbard's, thank you for giving me my first job and a home away from home. I love you guys! And thanks D for being nothing like Marnie. Love ya, Ma!

To all my crazy, fun loving friends growing up:

Aubrey, you are the true meaning of the word *friend*. I am so lucky to have someone like you in my life. I don't know how I'd get along without you. There's no one I'd rather be stuck with in traffic. Our friendship is the stuff of legends, at least I like to think so. Watch out for the tequila patch. Go Team Awesome!

Leanna, you are definitely one of my favorite people of all time. Through the laughter and the tears, still friends after all these years. I can't imagine growing up without you by my side. I'm so glad I still have you. From the days of all night Super Nintendo sleepovers and fort building, obsessing over Limp Bizkit and boys, to now, I wouldn't change a bit of it. Forever my best friend. I love you! Nobody drink the beer! The beer has gone bad!

Lisa and Lauren, the Little LA girls. Carpooling just isn't the same anymore. I love you two. I will never forget the fun we had, riding horses, rollerblading, playing Sardines... never play Sardines in the dark! I still have a scar. What are three girls to do for fun in a small town? Play in the dirt! That's what!

MaryAlice, I learned so much from our friendship. We sure had a lot of fun getting in and out of trouble. Thank you for being you.

Last, but certainly not least, thanks to all of you readers for picking up my books and giving me a chance. I hope you enjoy my work, and I look forward to entertaining you for years to come.

CHAPTER ONE

I suppose the first thing I should do is introduce myself. My name is Laverne. I know. Terrible, right? This is why I choose to go by L. Yes, I've seen *Laverne and Shirley*. Yes, I've been asked if I've seen that show a million and five times, and no, I don't know where Shirley is. I used to watch the reruns as a kid and actually found them quite enjoyable. It's a funny show, but still. I've been teased since birth for having such a, we'll say *unique* name, so I try to avoid that with the self-assigned nickname. When I tell strangers my name is L, they probably assume I said "Elle", which is fine by me, so long as no one says "Laverne". I was named after my grandmother, and I cannot stand it; the name, not my grandmother. I love my grandma. She's incredible. So I understand why my parents would want to name me after such a great person; but couldn't they have gone with her middle name, or maybe the name of another relative, or maybe even some outstanding, historical figure? I don't care; anything but Laverne. Again, I love my grandma, but it's not like it was a great honor for her to have a grandchild share her moniker. She doesn't even like the name. She makes everyone call her LaVee, which I think makes her sound more like some ultra hip, 90's dance-pop group than a little old white lady from Farber, Texas; but she is pretty fabulous, so LaVee suits her.

Of course, no matter how I tried to convince the world my name was L, the first day of school would always come around, and the first roll call, never fail, the teacher would give me away and call out "Jameson... Laverne Jameson..." and I would always raise my hand as my body sunk down in my seat, and I would say, "L. Please, call me L."

Kids teased me every so often when I was young, but in high school, things were a little different. It likely had a lot to do with the fact that we came from a teeny tiny town, and we'd all gone to school together since Kindergarten. Poking fun at the same things had become boring, especially since everyone had grown their own monumental teen-appropriate insecurities, making my name seem much less mock worthy. There was still the occasional first day, roll call snicker, but everyone had pretty much let it go.

Farber, Texas had to be the smallest town in the universe. At least it felt like it was. Though I was itching to get as far away from there as possible, I didn't have any sort of a plan in place. Graduation sort of snuck up on me, and I hadn't applied to many colleges outside the county. Okay, I didn't apply to any, and graduation didn't sneak up on me so much as I slacked on the application process, which, come to find out, you should really get a start on during junior year. My parents were disappointed to say the least, especially since I was an only child and their only hope for a successful offspring. They did, however, find small comfort in the fact that I would get my undergrad courses out of the way at the nearby community college for a nominal fee, which I responsibly offered to pay for myself, versus spending the first two years burning through cash and student loans at a fancy university.

It's not that I wasn't smart; I always got A's and B's. I just lacked a certain motivation. Even though the walls of the town sometimes seemed to be closing in, I was pretty comfortable where I was. I had a job in a local diner, where I made enough to make my car payments, buy clothes here and there, and pay for the slightly more than occasional night out with my best friend, Leah, and/or my beautiful boyfriend, Greg.

Greg was 22. Being 18, I felt like I was super special dating a 22 year old. We'd met when I was 16, and he was 20. It seemed so adult of me to have an adult boyfriend. Looking back, I wonder what was wrong with him that he had to date a teenager. Sure, I was more mature than most girls, but I did enjoy a party, and that seemed to interfere with "life planning". I just figured Greg and I would save up and one day, move far, far away and have like ten kids, a silver SUV, and a giant house. I'm pretty sure my waitress gig and his super part time job as a stock boy at GasMart weren't actually going to make that dream accessible, but it seemed perfectly doable at the time. He lacked ambition too. He didn't finish high school, and he never bothered to try for a GED or consult anyone at the community college to explore his options like other people often did. Greg decided early on that if his parents never went on to higher education, he didn't have to either. His dad got lucky and inherited a fairly successful garage, where he learned everything about mechanics. Greg didn't see a need to follow in his father's footsteps. He was certain that he could get by on good looks and charm. Though he liked cars, he didn't want to learn about them or the business. I'm not really sure what he thought he would do for money the rest of his life, but I guess, in hindsight, I realize he was just extremely lazy. We all kind of were.

It's easy to fall into a rut in a place like Farber. Everyone dreams of getting out, but if you've never been outside, it's hard to picture yourself out there, so you kind of adopt a *why bother* attitude. It's boring, but it's comforting. It's painful, but it's home. It's just easy. I think my parents saw that in me, and it worried them. They always thought I was destined for greatness. They wanted me to see the world and make history. I think that's why they hated Greg. He wasn't going anywhere, and he definitely wasn't going to make any kind of history, although, he did win a beer pong tournament one year. Now that's something. Well, at the time it was. There was a ribbon involved and a twenty-five dollar cash prize, which he spent on more beer. Good times.

My class had just graduated, and the relief of summer vacation was now wafting over us. A few kids from my class got into colleges out of state and were preparing for life on the outside. Most of us, though, were working our regular jobs with no serious plans for the future. A lot of the class, like myself, had already decided they would enroll in classes at Mitchell Farber Community College when enrollment opened the end of summer, and the handful left was just planning on letting life run its course right there in Farber. There were only 46 of us, but it was the first class in seven years to all graduate together. We didn't have any dropouts or hold backs. We all made it, and that was something to be proud of. Like I said, Farber was easy, and it was really easy for people to fall behind and not have anyone notice. At least the college would be a change of pace, or rather, change of face. It was the only community college within miles of us and the neighboring two towns, so people from out of town attended classes there.

My best friend since Kindergarten, Leah, was going to the MFCC with me. She and I made a plan to take all of our courses together. Neither of us had any clue what to major in, so we had mapped out our first semester with general education requirements. We had a stack of brochures and course outlines, and we were prepared. Maybe for the first time in a long time, we had a plan. Even though early enrollment was over two months down the road, we at least had that much figured out.

We had a pretty great plan for the summer too. I would work, as usual, and Leah would hang around, as usual, and we would party at night, as usual.

A week after graduation, I started my new schedule at the diner. I was now free for the next few months, so I was working five days a week instead of two or three. It was okay. It was pretty dead in the afternoons, and we only picked up for a couple hours during dinner. I liked the quiet, although I probably could have tolerated more customers for the tips. I wasn't exactly raking it in on that shift. In fact, I was the only one on from twelve to three, and then a second waitress came in to help with the "dinner rush", which only split my tips in half and annoyed me. I definitely could have handled more. Of course, being that I didn't have much ambition at the time, I never complained or did anything about it. I always just let it roll off. Besides, it wasn't like I was going anywhere anytime soon. I had a few hundred in savings, and, I figured, by the end of summer, I'd have a few hundred more. It would be just enough to pay for classes, books, and some new school clothes. I always had to have new clothes for the first day. Everything else I made went to my car and, well, like I said before, partying.

There was no one in the restaurant. The cook was outside smoking. He was always outside. I had to go get him when we had customers. I was making myself busy in the back booths doing my "side work", filling the salt and pepper shakers, primping the artificial sweeteners and whatnot, when the bells on the front door jingled. Whenever I was slow like this, and I heard that jingle, I had two thoughts, and it seemed kind of strange that they would both occur to me a the same time. One thought was *Damn! I don't want to fake nice and wait on anybody!* and the other thought was *Yay! Tips!* I put on my super happy, smiley face and walked around the corner, toward the front. My face immediately changed back to normal when I saw my best friend standing there, smacking her gum, with her hands in the pockets of her way too short cut offs. Again, two thoughts... *Damn! I could've used some extra money right about now* and *Oh good. I don't have to do anything.*

"Dude!" Leah said. "What are you doing?"

"Working," I said, laughing.

"Yeah right." She giggled and followed me over to the counter, where she took a seat. I stood behind it and leaned against the countertop.

"What have you been doing all day?" I asked my overly lip glossed friend.

"Oh, you know... nothing. Hey! There's a party tonight on the mountain. We should get Greg to take us up in his truck. Think he'd go for it?"

"Mountain party? Definitely. I'll ask him." I grabbed the smart phone that I got for my birthday in May out of my green apron pocket and started thumbing away at the qwerty keys. It was so smart that it often spoke for me and texted things I didn't intend. Auto spell turned one of the words into something completely different, so I had to text twice, but Greg got the idea. He sent me back a text that said something along the lines of *Shizz Yeah!* something he would say, and it looked like we were on.

"Yay!" I reported to Leah. "We're a go."

"Cool. Wanna come over before and get ready at my place?" Her place meaning in her room with the large mirrors on her closet doors.

"Sure. I'll call my mom and let her know I won't be home, and I'll come over after work. Can I borrow something to wear?"

"Duh. I have an extra sleeping bag for you too. See you tonight." She jumped off her bar stool and trotted off toward the door. The bells jingled behind her.

Mountain parties were always a lot of fun. There weren't exactly tons of mountains surrounding Farber, but there was one small mountain range to the West, where people went camping and hiking all the time. We would drive up to this campsite on top of Harper Mountain and sit around a campfire, drinking whatever we could get a hold of and socializing. Most of us, being the responsible people we were, would bring sleeping bags and either sleep in tents, or, on summer nights like these, sleep in the bed of a truck. A lot of the kids would pull the switcheroo and say they were sleeping at so and so's house, and then so and so would say they were sleeping at someone else's house, but I had an honesty policy with my parents. They knew I partied, but they knew I would never drink and drive or drive home with someone who had been drinking, so they figured as long as they knew where I was, and I checked in every so often on my cell phone, they were typically okay with me staying out all night. Cool, huh? I guess it was the *well they're gonna do it anyway so they might as well be educated and safe about it* theory. At least I never had to sneak out or lie about what I was doing. I think that it actually helped me make better decisions... sometimes. I always had their voices in my head: *We trust you, L.* It didn't always stop me from doing foolish things, but I'd say nine out of ten, it kept me from going overboard. Leah didn't have that voice. She always told her mom she was sleeping at my house, and she would really be at these parties, drunk as humanly possible, chain smoking, and hanging all over whoever was interested. Her mom never bothered to call my house to check. She had five other kids at home, split between a few different fathers, and a truck driver boyfriend to keep her busy. She was a really nice lady, just a little lost. Leah seemed a little lost too, wandering from guy to guy.

I'm not calling Leah a super skank or anything. She was just a little more free with herself than some, which I found kind of strange since she had just started having sex junior year. We had this pact. We were going to wait, and whoever did it first had to eat dog poop. Well, I kind of lost, and I decided not to tell her right away. Losing your virginity is of course something you would want to share with your best friend ASAP. Except, I really didn't want to eat dog excrement, and Leah was the kind of girl who would take a mile if given an inch. I knew once I told her I had done it, she would go right out and do it too, and I didn't want her first time to be cheapened just because she wanted to jump on the ban wagon or whatever. My first time was with Greg on Valentine's Day my junior year. Cliché, I know, but it was pretty special. Plus, we'd been dating a whole eight months already, which in teen years is like a million, so it seemed right. I wanted to tell Leah the second it happened, but I waited almost a whole month before letting it slip out. She didn't make me eat dog poop, but I was right about the other part.

The very same night I told her I slept with Greg, she went out and had sex with a random, out-of-towner at a party we went to. In her defense, he was really, really good looking, but neither of us knew his last name, and we never did find out. It wasn't exactly the special moment every girl dreams about. She sure seemed proud of herself though, like she was part of a special club. I didn't have the heart to tell her that being a member didn't really make you any cooler. I mean, Greg was the only guy I'd ever been with. He was the only guy I thought I'd be with for the rest of my life. Since the night Leah lost her virginity, she'd already been with most of the decent looking guys in town, and even some of the not so decent ones. She'd never really had a boyfriend, and she was quickly getting a reputation. I knew it bothered her, but she didn't want to talk about it. Of course, every time we'd go to a party, and she'd have a random hookup, the next morning, she would swear off boys and alcohol, but that would only last until the next party. At least she was safe. Well, as safe as one can be, hopping around like that. She was on the pill and always had protection handy. I even convinced her to go to the clinic and get tested a couple times. So far, so good, I guess. I really did try to talk to her about it, but she always had something flippant or funny to say, so I tried not to let it bug me too much. I loved her, and I just wanted her to be happy. We always had a good time.

Nine o'clock was taking an eternity to come around. We closed at nine, and we couldn't start our closing cleanup until quarter 'til, and that was only if we didn't have any customers. I couldn't wait to get out of there and over to Leah's house. I checked the clock again; *8:30*. I rolled my eyes and looked over to Ben. Ben, as usual, was sitting in a booth, playing with his cell phone. He was the owner's son, and he rarely worked there. Ben was usually only there to substitute for someone else. He had come in as the second on the shift because the usual girl, Stacey, called out sick. Though I didn't really care for Ben or his super lax attitude, I knew he would want to go to the mountain as well, which would be a plus when cleaning up because that meant instead of watching me do everything to close up, he would actually pitch in so he could get out of there faster, or so I thought. I watched him thumbing away at his cell phone and rolled my eyes again. Back to the clock; *8:31*. Great.

Bored, I ran my tongue over the inside of my left cheek. There was a lump where I had bitten the inside of my cheek two days before. It still hurt like crazy, but for some reason I couldn't leave it alone. I'm not sure why I would do that; it just makes it worse, but I've always done that. I think maybe everyone does. I don't know.

I decided to finish up my side work, which turned into me finishing up all the side work and prepping for close myself. Ben didn't help at all, but I didn't complain. At least having all the extra stuff to do made the time seem to go a little faster.

The clock finally hit 8:52. *Yes!* Just a few more minutes, and we would have that neon sign turned off, and we'd be out of there. Just as I was admiring the advance in time, I heard the familiar jingle of the door opening.

NO!!!! I screamed in my head as I turned with my biggest, fakest smile ever. I tried my best to mask my annoyance as I greeted the man who had just thrown a giant wrench into my fun plan. *Ugh! Not this guy.* I knew this guy. He was a giant pain. He was one of the grumpiest customers I'd ever had the displeasure of serving, and even though he complained constantly and never left more than a three percent tip, he kept coming back. He was there almost every night, usually earlier than this.

"Hi," I said with a huge smile. "Your usual table?"

The man just grunted and scowled at me as I escorted him toward his favorite seat in the back. As we passed the counter, the cook peered out from the pass through window and frowned. He didn't want to be there any more than I did.

I placed a menu on the table as I normally did. He always ordered the same thing, yet every time, he took five minutes glossing over the entire menu before ordering. I don't think he even read it; I'm pretty sure he did it just to draw out the miserable experience even more. I always wondered why he was the way he was. No one could be that bitter and have such a need to spread the gloom without some kind of past trauma or heartache. I tried my best to imagine that he was wounded somehow, and his sour exterior was just a front for his pain. Otherwise, I couldn't have been nice to him. If I didn't excuse his behavior with a mental reminder every time, *this guy needs compassion*, I probably would have thrown a drink or two at him at some point. Throwing a drink on someone is something I'd always wanted to do actually, but I never acted on it at work. Although, I probably should have thrown a few things at Ben.

As I walked back toward the wait station to fetch Mr. Happy some water, Ben pranced on over and joined me at the pitchers.

"Hey, so, uh, you got this, right? I'm gonna hit the light for ya, and I'm gonna take off, okay?" Ben said.

"Ben. Seriously?"

"L... it's not like there's anything left to do. I'll let you take it. You should get the tip," he said as if it were some big prize. The thirty-two cent tip. How nice. "I'll take the stragglers next time," he continued, "promise." He pranced off toward the front window to turn off the neon beacon. If only he had decided to do that at 8:52.

"Oh, and hey," he said coming back around, "I'm gonna take a twenty from the register; just tell my mom to run her credit card for twenty when she gets here to balance the till.

Okay, thanks!"

I just shrugged and shook my head. It wasn't as if he was going to actually let me respond or give me an option. He was already out the door. His mom would be there soon to count the drawer and settle the credit cards.

I returned to my sour faced customer and let him grumble about a water spot on his glass. I finally got his order, and it was the same thing he always ordered, a plain cheeseburger with fries, extra crispy. Given that he did every other time he came in there, I already knew that he would later be complaining that the fries weren't crispy enough and his burger had no flavor. The fries really couldn't get any crispier without becoming ash, and the cook would put extra seasoning on this guy's patties just to make a point, so we all knew he complained just to be a menace. Maybe he got a kick out of it. Maybe in his home life he was a jovial sunshine maker, but I doubt it.

At long last, he was on his slow crawl out the door when Marnie, the owner, finally showed up. She was late. I glanced at the clock; *9:20*. Then I glanced over at the dirty table and saw my thirty-two cent tip stacked in the usual way at the edge of the tabletop.

"Where's Ben?" Marnie asked as she scanned the empty restaurant.

"He left. He took twenty from the register and wanted me to ask you to..."

"Okay." She sighed and pulled a twenty from her pocket. "So, where was he off to?"

"He's going up to the mountain tonight." I didn't have to cover for him. Marnie knew her son partied. She didn't seem to mind a bit. She actually seemed oddly proud of it.

"Oh. The mountain. Fun. Did he finish his side work?"

"No, I finished up for him. No big deal," I lied. It was a huge deal in my head. I hated doing his share for him. He was spoiled.

"Well, boys will be boys," she said as she tossed her hair

behind her and chuckled.

Boys will be boys. I hated that phrase. She said it all the time. That was his excuse? He was allowed to slack off and act like a turd simply because he lucked out in the gender lottery? Ridiculous. I wasn't about to argue it; I wanted out of there. I rushed to the dirty table and cleared the dishes. I brought out a bar mop and new settings and finished cleaning. I checked the coffee pots; Off. I checked the soup station; All clear and turned off. I grabbed the vacuum from the stock closet, plugged it in, and raced around the carpet as quickly as I could. I added my final ticket to the total I had already come up with from my previous tickets, and I was ready to go.

"Okay," I said, "so, I'll see ya tomorrow."

"Alright. Have a good night."

I turned to grab my bag from under the counter. I was untying my apron from the back and almost to the back door when Marnie hollered from the front.

"Wait! L!"

Crap! "Yeah?" I responded, coming back.

"Can you get the flag for me and the stuff from outside?"

I had forgotten the stuff from outside. Like she couldn't have done it herself. It was my job, but still. Ben left before we even closed, and she was twenty minutes late, and I couldn't wait to get to Leah's. I looked at the clock again; *9:40.*

I went outside and dropped the flag down from the pole, careful not to let it touch the ground. I folded it myself, which is not easy to do properly by the way. I stacked the plastic chairs from around the two outside tables and placed the plastic tablecloths on top of them. I brought them all back through the front door and put them off to the side for the girl who would open the next morning.

"Sorry," I said as I walked back toward Marnie at the register.

"That's okay," she said, sounding a little annoyed. Then she continued sweetly, "have a good night. See you tomorrow."

I was kind of pissed that she was irritated. Again, Ben didn't do jack all night, but boys will be boys or whatever.

I was free! I ran to my car and sped off toward Leah's house. I finally got there. It was just before ten, and I was super on edge. I hated being rushed to get ready. As I walked toward her front door, my phone chirped. It was a text from Greg. He was running behind too. He was going on a beer run with his buddies, and then he had to go pick up his friend Jeremy. He said he'd try to hurry, but I knew that meant they'd be at least an hour. That was fine by me. It gave me time to fix myself up and unwind a little.

"Finally!" Leah said as she swung open her front door.

I stepped in to see two of her sisters and her little brother sitting on the couch, involved in a kiddie movie. Her mom was in the kitchen, making popcorn for the little terrors. They looked sweet staring at the television, but when they weren't preoccupied by dancing pigs or singing rabbits, they were wild.

"Hi, Lana!" I shouted back toward the kitchen.

"Oh, hi, L!" she yelled back.

"Shhh!" the three couch monkeys hissed in unison.

"Oops," I whispered, "sorry."

I followed Leah around the corner to her room. She had her makeup set up in front of the large closet door mirror. Becca, her fifteen year old sister, was testing out the different shades of lipstick.

"Move over, Becks," Leah ordered, joining her sister on the floor in front of the mirror.

"I'm done anyway," Becca said, checking herself in the mirror one last time and smacking her lips together. "Hey, L, look what I got today." Becca ran over to her bed and grabbed a magazine off the comforter.

"Oh, yeah," Leah squealed, jumping up from the carpet,

"check this out." She met her sister in between the two beds. They shared a room, so it was a good thing they shared similar interests too.

"Brick Donovan!" Becca revealed as she held up the magazine.

It was a gorgeous photo of our obsession, rock star Brick Donovan. His blue eyes leapt off the page. Every time I saw a new picture of him, I felt a heaviness in my whole body; an aching. He was so beautiful, and he was incredibly talented. We were completely and totally in love with him. Sure I had Greg, but Brick was different. He was like a god. He was unattainable, untouchable, which made us want him even more. His pictures were plastered all over my room. Lana didn't let Becca and Leah put holes in or use tape on her walls, so they had a binder full of cutouts and clippings. Looking at the cover, I knew I had to get a copy of this magazine for myself. I already knew exactly where I would tack up this magnificent cover page.

"Oh wow," I said as I reached for the magazine.

"No, wait," Becca turned it back toward herself. "It gets better."

I sighed impatiently as I watched Becca finger the pages of the magazine. I wanted it in my hands. I wanted Brick in my hands.

"Look at this," she said giddily as she swung the magazine back toward me.

I gasped as I gazed upon the beauty. It was a centerfold of the entire band, Brick Party Sundae, with the breathtakingly gorgeous Brick Donovan at the front of the pack.

"I know, right?" Leah added excitedly. She giggled at my wide eyes.

"I have to get this. I need one," I said, already planning a trip to the market in my head for first thing in the morning.

"The article is awesome too," Becca said. "He is so deep. You have to read it. You'll just die."

"Later," Leah replied for me. "We have to get ready."

I looked at the magazine longingly. I wanted to read that article; I had to. Leah looked at me, annoyed, and I knew it really did have to wait 'til later. I snapped back to reality and remembered we had a party to get to. That psyched me up again.

"Can I borrow something to wear?" I asked Leah. I didn't want to go to the party smelling like biscuits and bleach water, wearing my black slacks and white blouse uniform; not exactly sexy.

Leah opened her closet up for me and motioned for me to go ahead. The nights had been ridiculously hot, and there'd undoubtedly be a campfire at the mountain, so I grabbed a red cropped t-shirt I'd borrowed before and a pair of jeans. Lucky for the both of us, we were both a size five and had nearly the same style. We'd basically doubled our wardrobe by sharing all the time. People often confused us for sisters since we kind of looked alike, both of us with long dark hair and brown eyes; and being inseparable since Kindergarten, we'd adopted the same kind of mannerisms. We liked that people thought we were related. We were close like family. Leah had siblings, but I was an only child, and she was the sister I always wanted. When I wasn't at work or with Greg, I was guaranteed to be with Leah. L Squared we were called. Leah and Laverne, the two Ls. L^2. Mathematically, I realize, it doesn't make any kind of sense to be L^2; it should have been L times 2, or L plus L, but L Squared just sounded cooler when we came up with it, and no one ever seemed to catch the equation flub. We even had our own handshake; a high five, then a low five, a fist bump, then blow it up, and then we'd put our left index fingers and thumbs in the shape of an L and put them together to make a square. Okay, again with the technicalities; technically the shape we made with our fingers was a rectangle, but we still yelled "L Squared" when we did it. Yes, we were dorks, but we didn't care.

I changed into the clothes I had chosen from Leah's

closet and sat next to her at the mirror. She had waited for me to start her makeup. We always did makeup together. I checked my phone. Nothing from Greg. It had only been ten minutes since his text, so I knew he wouldn't be there for a while. We had plenty of time for makeup, hair, and gossip.

"Pass me the good eyeliner." Leah pointed toward her favorite liner, but I already knew which one she wanted. "We're doing smokey eyes, right?"

"Sure," I said. Leah was great at the smokey look. I always had her do my eye shadow for me. I was bound to mess it up somehow, and the look would go from smokey to smudgy if I did it myself. I finished my foundation, did my lips, and waited for Leah to get done so she could do my eyes.

"So," she said, squinting as she applied her mascara, "do you think Bryan will be there tonight?" Bryan was a popular guy who had graduated a couple years ahead of us. He was going to college in Arizona, but we'd heard he would be home for the summer.

"I don't know. I think he's back."

"I heard he broke up with Gina," Leah said. Gina was Bryan's girlfriend all through high school. She got a scholarship to some big school in California, and apparently, the distance was doing some harm to their relationship.

"No way," I said.

"Yep. And... she's not coming back for summer break. She's got some internship thingy in California, so she won't be around."

I could see a plan hatching in Leah's head. She finished her face and turned to me with eye shadow in hand.

"So," I said coyly, "are you gonna..."

"Oh, I don't know. If he's there, we'll see."

We giggled at the thought. She'd had a crush on him since we were freshman and he was a junior; a lot of girls had crushes on him, but he was always with Gina.

"Close," Leah said. I closed my eyes, and she started

brushing on the colors. I felt her blending my left eye. "Open," she said, inspecting my eyes. "Okay, close," she said again, this time blending my right eye. "Alright, open." Her eyes darted back and forth as she closely surveyed my makeup. "Looks good."

I looked over into the mirror. It did look good. She always did a nice job. I liked it. I looked sultry. That's kind of a silly word for me. I wasn't really the sultry, sexy kind, but I sure could look like it if I wanted to.

"Thanks," I said, approving of her work.

"What are you doing with your hair?" she said.

"Crap." I had kind of forgotten about my hair. It was up in a ponytail. I guess the makeup looked good enough, I wasn't really concerned with my hair. A ponytail is a pretty juvenile look though. I pulled the tie out of my hair and tousled my follicles with my hands. It was a disaster. I checked my phone again. It looked like there was enough time to fix the mess. Leah's hair had already been straightened perfectly. She was ready to go.

"Can I use your straightener?" I got up to head for the bathroom.

"Yes, please do." She laughed. "It's still plugged in. Turn it off when you're done."

I hurried into the bathroom and checked the straightener for heat. It was still hot. I ran it over the different sections of my hair, watching the nasty kink from my ponytail quickly disappear. I stepped back and looked at the final result. It was a vast improvement from the mess I was when I walked in the house that night. I looked ready to party down. I flipped off the straightener and pulled the plug from the socket. I squirted some hair shine goop from a bottle in the medicine cabinet and worked it through my strands. All better. I waltzed back into Leah and Becca's room with confidence.

"Ooh," Leah exclaimed, "much better." She winked at me and laughed.

Becca looked up from her magazine and nodded in

approval. She was still completely involved in the Brick Party Sundae article. Knowing her, she'd probably read it twenty times that day. She memorized every single piece of Brick trivia that ever was. Can't blame her; I did it too.

Leah was also guilty of the insanity. She had a crazy Brick obsession too. At one point, she dropped almost ninety dollars in an online auction for a Brick Donovan signed photo. She'd been saving the money from babysitting jobs for like forever, and then she blew it all on one photo of Brick. Worth it? Definitely. He was the absolute, and I was pretty jealous she had something in her possession that he'd once touched.

We checked ourselves over one more time and then retired to Leah's bed and sprawled out over the comforter, waiting for a text or a phone call from Greg. We talked a bunch of nonsense and laughed like giddy little kids until my phone chirped again. Greg was outside.

"Have a good night, little sis," Leah said to Becca as we exited the room. Becca stuck her tongue out in protest. She knew we were going to a party, but she was still too young to get an invite.

"Okay, Mom, we're going to that movie now," Leah lied.

"What time will you girls be back?" Lana quizzed.

"We're staying at L's house tonight. I'll be home in the morning."

"Oh, okay. Have fun," Lana said.

We all said goodbye, and then L Squared was out the door. We got in my car and had Greg follow us around the corner. I couldn't leave my car outside Leah's house in case her mom looked outside at some point and noticed it. We parked and piled into the back of Greg's crew cab. Greg's buddy, Jeremy, was sitting shotgun, so we had to get in the back. I always thought Jeremy and Leah would have made a cute couple, but for some reason neither of them was interested in that idea. I guess they knew each other too well or something.

Jeremy had already been drinking. He smelled like booze and would not stop laughing and talking about, well, nothing really. He lit a cigarette, which was sort of cruel since the air from his window was just blowing the smoke right in my face. I smoked occasionally, more often when I was drinking, but I didn't really care for second hand. I hated smelling like cigarettes. I could feel my hair getting blasted with the scent of burning tobacco. I clutched the perfume I had stashed in my purse, ready to spray myself down as soon as the smoking was over. It didn't really matter since we'd all smell like a campfire soon enough anyway, but I was still inclined to be a total girl about it. Jeremy reached into a plastic bag with his free hand and passed a bottle back to us. Leah gladly accepted the offering and took a giant swig from the brand new bottle.

She handed it over to me. I inspected the label in the glow of the street lights. It was a pretty decent whiskey. Jeremy must have sprung for it. Greg never got anything but bottom shelf liquor, the kind that assaulted your body and burned your esophagus. I took a large drink myself and then another before passing it back to Leah. She took one more giant swig then handed it to me for one more. I quickly took my third and passed it back over the seat for Jeremy to stow away. I checked around us for other cars and cops; no one. I looked over the seat and saw the speedometer. Greg was driving carefully and was just one mph above the speed limit.

Another half hour and we were at the campsite. As we pulled up, I saw that there was already a pretty big crowd forming around the campfire. There were four trucks backed up in a half circle, and people were sitting on the tailgates. The rest of the cars and trucks were parking along the side of the campground. We were the seventh vehicle there. Greg parked us a little further down, near an outhouse. We would be sleeping in his truck, and he knew that with my bladder and how much I would be drinking, I would need immediate access to that outhouse at some point during the night. He was so thoughtful.

As he turned the ignition off, I started to really feel the effects of the liquor. My lips and my nose got sort of numb, my vision was slightly fuzzy, and I was warm all over. It felt nice, like a big soft sweater hug. I smiled to myself. I looked over at Leah. She looked pretty happy too.

"Should we do one more?" she asked, knowing I'd say yes. She was already motioning to Jeremy to give her the bottle.

He was a little slow to react, but he eventually got us what we were asking for. I spun the top off and took a drink. As I winced and opened my mouth to let out the sting, I handed the bottle over to my friend, who mimicked the action.

We got out of the truck, and our eyes automatically began scanning the group by the fire. We squinted as we tried to see the faces of the people who had gathered. Even with my drunk-o-vision, I could still tell who everyone was, probably because the faces were all so familiar. It was always the same people. Everyone in town between the ages of seventeen and twenty two were regulars at the campsite.

This site and the neighboring two sites would always fill up before midnight. We never got hassled by the cops, which is sort of surprising since I'm sure they knew about these parties. No one ever drove home though; everyone camped, so I guess it wasn't really a priority. They could have probably gotten quite a few of us for underage drinking, but that would require them making the drive all the way up the mountainside, and the local cops weren't exactly motivated. Every once in a while, a park ranger would come through and make sure the fires were well structured. He would flirt with the girls, crack a few jokes, and be back on his way.

As I searched the faces in the crowd from behind the truck, I noticed someone different; familiar, but not part of the usual crowd. His back was to me, but he turned to the left, and his profile was lit up by the glow of the fire. It was Bryan. He looked handsome as ever. He was wearing a fitted shirt, which showed off his super fit, college athlete body. I skipped around to Leah.

"Leah!" I whisper-squealed. "He's here! He's here!"

"Where?"

"There," I motioned with my head.

She grabbed my arm and squeezed it to convey her excitement.

"Who's here? What?" Greg came up behind me and slipped his arms around my waist.

"Nobody. Nothing. Never mind." I giggled.

"Whatever. Girls." Greg shook his head and grabbed my hand to lead me to the crowd. He knew whoever I was talking about had to be for Leah's benefit, so he didn't really care.

Leah skipped next to us. Jeremy had gone in search of a tree far enough away so as to have some privacy. I'm not sure why the guys always insisted on peeing in trees and bushes when there was a perfectly good outhouse just yards away. I guess it's a guy thing.

The three of us came up on the campfire and greeted the crowd. We took a spot close to Bryan so Leah and I could observe the situation and come up with a plan. So far, there weren't any girls attached to his immediate group. He stood, beer in hand, with three other guys. I winked at Leah, and she giggled, stealing a glance at Bryan's backside. Greg was oblivious to the whole thing. He knew Bryan's older brother Charlie, who was also part of the group next to us. Greg went over to the guys, joined in their conversation, and grabbed a beer from their cooler. Greg was always grabbing things out of people's coolers, or refrigerators, or ice buckets, or whatever was handy at the time. I never really thought about it before, but he really was a rude, self-entitled jackass. Anyway, he guzzled the beer like he owned it and grabbed another. The guys didn't seem to care, and maybe they really didn't. It was kind of a free for all at these parties. We all brought stuff, and we all shared; too bad Greg never brought anything to contribute. He would buy cheap booze and keep it stashed in the truck for himself, going back for a secret swig every now and then during pee breaks. I, on the other hand, was the go to cigarette girl. I always gave away more than I smoked. Drunk people would run out and bum them from me. I didn't mind. I was happy to share. Like I said, I wasn't really a big smoker anyway; I just always had them on me in case the mood struck. Leah and I would buy cartons together and split them. She smoked the majority of hers, and mine mostly ended up in the fingertips of others.

"Hey! We have some jungle juice over here! Grab a cup!" a hyper and friendly voice yelled toward us. It was Amanda. Amanda was a super friendly, overly bubbly girl we'd known pretty much since forever. She wasn't really one of our close friends, but for some reason, she thought she was. In truth, she was nice and all, but she was super annoying. It required a lot of energy and patience to hang out with her, so we tried not to if we could help it.

The girl spoke with a ridiculously thick, valley girl accent. No one knew quite where she picked it up, being that no one else we knew talked like that, and she grew up in the same town we did. She sounded like a beach bunny, bobble head, and she acted like one too. She was really cute. I'll give her that. She had long, wavy blonde hair, a tiny waist, and huge boobs. On top of being super great looking, she was known to be pretty easy. Guys loved her, and girls were mostly jealous of her, but Leah and I genuinely just couldn't stand her. At least that's how I felt; Leah said she didn't really care, but, looking back, she might have actually been a little jealous like the rest of female population. They were usually in direct competition for the same guys. We weren't the types to be mean though, at least I wasn't anyway, so we always played nice and visited with her at social events.

"Oh my god!" Amanda continued, drawn out in valley

speak. "I love your shoes!" She pointed to Leah's sneakers.

"Thanks," Leah said, obviously feigning sweetness. "You told me that the last two times I saw you too."

I ribbed her with my elbow and gave her a sideways glance.

"Well," Amanda said, completely missing the catty tone of the remark, "I still totally love them. You have the best style. Here!" She offered up her hand to take Leah's cup and fill it.

"Thanks," Leah said more politely. "I'm glad you still like them. I like your..." she scanned Amanda up and down searching for something to compliment, "earrings. They're pretty."

"Oh my god! Thank you!" Amanda cooed, handing a full cup back to Leah and grabbing for mine. "I got them at that new store, uh, you know, the one over on..." she trailed off, and her head tilted slightly in thought. "Wait. What was I saying?"

Amanda did that often. She would stop mid-sentence or mid-story and completely blank on what she was talking about. It fit the whole fake accent thing, but we weren't sure if the situational amnesia was an act or if she really did lack retention and conversation skills. She always got straight A's in school, so we knew she didn't lack intelligence. The whole daft girl thing had to be for show. Maybe she thought it was cute. Guys sure did.

"You were telling us where you got those earrings," Leah reminded her.

"Oh! Right! Duh!" Amanda laughed. "That store. The new one." And she was done.

"Oh... the new one." Leah looked at me like she was in agony.

"Cool," I said, "we'll have to check it out."

"So," Amanda continued on a new subject, "did you guys see Bryan? Holy hotness! Like whoa. Somebody's been working out."

27

Leah looked at me again, this time a little more annoyed. I could see she felt threatened.

"Yeah," I stepped in. "Where's his girlfriend?" I knew he wasn't with Gina anymore, but I had to say something to try and divert Amanda's interest.

"Oh, they broke up!" Amanda cheered.

Leah looked at me and rolled her eyes. I knew what she was thinking. She was going to have to compete with Amanda for Bryan's attention.

"Oh!" Amanda shrieked. "Have you guys met my boyfriend?"

Boyfriend? Our ears perked up. Could it be the competition had just come to a halt?

"Travis! Travis! Come here for a sec!" She called over toward the herd around Bryan. A good looking guy with a serious tan and gorgeous green eyes came forward with a smile. We didn't recognize him as one of the guys we'd gone to school with. He joined us and put his arm around Amanda. They looked really great together; him being a muscular guy with perfect features, and her being this tiny little thing with perfect everything.

"What's up, ladies? I'm Travis." He stuck one of his giant, no doubt football catching hands out to greet us. We each shook his hand, and he flashed a killer smile. His wavy, blonde hair glistened in the glow of the fire. They looked like Ken and Barbie. The thought made me laugh aloud a little, but luckily no one noticed. "I'm sooo wasted," he said with a strange hint of a valley accent; it was kind of a toned down version of Amanda's. This made sense.

"Travey, here, is visiting from Cali. We met last week. His grandparents live next door. Isn't that awesome? I'm going back with him in a few days, and we're totally gonna rage it up this summer at the beach. Right, boo?" Amanda looked at him longingly. I was stuck on the fact that she just called him "boo".

"No doubt! It's gonna be sick!" He smiled wide and

kissed Amanda on the forehead.

"Wow," I said, partially stunned. "That is really awesome. You'll have so much fun."

"Yeah, obvi," she said, robbing the word *obviously* of its two other syllables. "It is the sunshine state or whatever. We'll have the best time."

"Obvi," I repeated, trying not to laugh. Part of me was a little jealous that this girl was actually getting out of town, and the other part of me was trying not to break out in a giggle fit over their odd display and choice of vocabulary.

I glanced over at Leah from the corner of my eye, and I could see she was trying hard to keep a straight face also.

Travis pulled on Amanda's shirt hem and motioned for her to join him back over where the guys were. He was just visiting, but he seemed to be getting along really well with everybody. He was interesting, kind of.

"Looks like we're heading that way," Amanda said, giving into his silent request. "Coming?"

"Uh," I paused, looking to Leah for a signal. She widened her eyes a little like she needed a minute. "We'll be there in a sec."

"Toats! Go ahead and take as much JJ as you want," Amanda said. Then she and Travis trotted off toward the group. It always took so much energy to talk to this girl. It required actual listening and comprehension. *Toats?* I guess she meant totally. *JJ*, I suppose, was her nickname for the jungle juice. I'm not exactly fluent in Amanda speak, and I'm pretty sure that's something to be grateful for.

"Whoa," Leah said as the twosome walked away. "She's like toats weird."

"Obvi," I replied. We cracked up laughing. "And isn't *Florida* the sunshine state?"

"Uh, yeah," Leah answered with satisfaction. Amanda had once again proven herself to be comically entertaining.

"Well, at least she's not after Bryan," I pointed out.

"Yes, and that is the important thing."

"Are you gonna go say hi?" I quizzed.

"Uh... maybe a little more liquid courage first. Creeper?" Leah asked as she reached for the nozzle on the side of the cooler to pour herself some more alcoholic punch. We both downed two more cups. It tasted like fruit; the alcohol was masked by the infusion of juice flavors. I guess that's why we always referred to jungle juice as "creeper". It was a mix of three or four different hard liquors with a delightful juice and fruit additive that somehow concealed the taste of the alcohol. It was super easy going down, too easy, and then the liquor would all of a sudden creep up on you. We were always slammed before we knew it. You'd think we'd take it easy then on the stuff, but it tasted so good, and since we were never exactly sure how strong it was, we always went a tad overboard.

Leah, having drank all the courage she needed, decided to finally go over and talk to Bryan. I wished her luck, checked her lip gloss, and walked with her over to the guys. My boyfriend was dominating the conversation, telling everyone about his ultimate defeat earlier that day when he outran a sports car with his truck in town. He was a proud peacock, puffing out his chest and making tire squeal noises for dramatic effect.

"I dusted him," Greg concluded.

"That's like sick to the face, man!" Amanda's boyfriend cheered as he put up his right hand for a high five with Greg.

Leah mouthed *sick to the face* to me as if she couldn't believe what she'd just heard. I just shrugged. I wasn't familiar with the term. It must have been a "sunshine state" thing. I shouldn't be so hard on them I guess. Leah and I had our own code, and we used slang quite often, but they just seemed like such easy targets at the time. They sure made fun gossip material for later. I mean, if anyone ever saw us doing our L Squared handshake, they'd have thought we were ridiculous. It's always easy to judge others before you judge yourself. Terrible, sure, but fun, definitely.

"Dude, it was sweet. He was obliterated!" Greg went on. See what I mean? My boyfriend didn't exactly have the vocabulary of an ace scholar either, but I still thought he was perfect and could do no wrong.

"That's awesome, baby," I said as I rubbed his back. The guys all nodded in our direction to acknowledge we'd joined the powwow.

"Oh my god!" Amanda chimed in. "I have the most brill idea! You guys should race some time." She waved her finger between Greg and Travis. "Travey has the hottest car. It would be wicked fun."

"Wow, that is brill," I offered, assuming brill meant brilliant. "But aren't you guys taking off soon? Bummer. Guess that's not gonna happen. Rain check?" The last thing I wanted was to encourage my Gregory to partake in mindless, self-indulgent, boy behavior that could ultimately end up in injury or police interference.

"Sure! Wait, what?" Amanda asked, her face twisting up in confusion as it often seemed to do.

I couldn't tell if she had forgotten what she was saying again, or if she really didn't understand what I had just said. I glared back at her blank stare, waiting for it to click.

"Oh, right," she finally said. "Rain check. For sure!"

I was amazed that with her extensive knowledge of made up words she got stuck on the common phrase "rain check". As I pondered the uselessness of this entire conversation, I felt the creeper sneak up through my body. All of my muscles grew incredibly warm, and my vision fuzzed out even more than it had before. It felt nice, but I knew the sway was coming, so I wrapped my arm around Greg's and sort of propped myself against his side to steady myself.

"Dude," Greg addressed Travis, "so what kind of car do you have?"

Their words became a muddle. It was partly because I was drunk, but it was mostly because car talk was like a foreign language. I always wished I was that cool chick who knew all about trucks, and lift kits, and muscle cars, but it seemed incredibly time consuming to actually learn about cars, so I never really did. Instead of the cool chick, I was the girl at the service station every three to four months being told she not only needs her oil changed, but that she also needs a plethora of expensive services done, half of which sounded made up or unnecessary, but who wants to be stranded on the side of the road because the catamaranadingdong fell apart, and the car caught on fire? Not me. Yeah, I should have taken a mechanics class or something.

As the boys talked, I noticed Leah staring down her mark. Bryan was trying to pretend he was interested in the car talk, but I could tell he was bored. I nudged her. She looked at me, took a deep breath, and went in for a greeting. She said hello; he said hello. They started talking about how much he loved college and how much she was looking forward to it. Before I knew it, they were walking away to find a quieter place to talk. The plan was in motion.

What seemed like ten minutes, but was probably more like an hour, later, Leah and Bryan made their way back to us. She was smiling wide, and he looked pretty happy too.

She ran up next to me and squeezed my arm.

"What happened?" I asked.

"We're going out. Tomorrow night. I'm so excited!"

"That's awesome. Did uh, anything else happen?" I elbowed her arm and winked.

"No. Lame," she scoffed as if it were an impossibility. "I'm not like that."

I looked at her sideways.

"Okay," she gave in, "maybe I am, but this is different. He says he really likes me, and he wants to get to know me. We're taking it slow."

"Aw. Leah's got a boyfriend."

"Shh!" she looked around coyly. "Whatever, L. Let's go

get another drink."

I never turned down a request like that, so off we went to drink some more. I looked around the campsite at all the glowing faces. Ben was there, but he didn't say hello. He just waved and then kind of ignored me all night. Go figure. All the usuals seemed to be in place, and a few people from out of town showed up. By the time two a.m. came around, the place was pretty full.

Leah and I just kept drinking. A few cups and two cigarettes later, we were pretty much wasted. We decided to call it good and piled into the truck to pass out. Greg stayed outside. He said he'd be there soon, but he didn't show up until almost five. I barely noticed though. I was so out of it, by the time he got back, I was pretty much dead to the world. I guess we took up too much space; me in the front seat and Leah in the back, so he crashed in the truck bed in a sleeping bag. Jeremy never made it back to the truck. At some point, I thought I remembered looking hazily out the window and seeing him slink into a tent.

I woke up the next morning with a disgusting and painfully familiar taste in my mouth. The remains of the alcohol were fuming up from my stomach and into my mouth, which already tasted a lot like the smell of an old ash tray, so I didn't really need the added taste of a distillery in there too. My head was swirling, and my stomach had a pit in it. I knew this feeling. I had to eat ASAP or risk the chance of vomiting the rest of the day. If I didn't feed my hangovers first thing, they'd turn into a lingering sickness that would stay with me the whole day. My mission was to wake our little party up, so we could get down the mountain and into a line at a drive thru.

"Leah," I whispered. "Leah, you awake?"

"No," she responded. "I'm dead. Bury me, and go away."

"Breakfast burritos sound amazing, right?"

"No. Sleep sounds amazing," she protested and grunted.

"Okay. I know... we'll get yummy breakfast burritos, and then you can sleep at my house, after a nice long shower." I thought the shower thing might work. She hated smelling like a booze fueled fire. Somehow, smelling like the night before makes hangovers feel worse.

"Shower?" The wheels were turning. "Ugh! Fine."

"Yay! I have to go find Greg and Jeremy, and then we're outta here!"

I opened the passenger side door and was immediately attacked by the sun. I shielded my eyes with my hand and smacked my lips together a couple times. I made my way around to the bed of the truck and saw Greg asleep with his jacket over his head. I pulled the jacket back and stroked his face.

"Babe?" I said quietly. "We need to go get food."

"Mmm..." he said, half interested. Then he perked up a little. "Food? Okay. Where's Jeremy?"

"I think he's in that one." I pointed to a pup tent. "Call him."

Greg sat up and got his cell phone out of his pants pocket. As the phone rang, he winced in pain. No one answered.

"Damn!" Greg said. "I didn't even hear it over there. Did you hear it?"

"No," I said. We couldn't leave without him, and I didn't want to be knocking on tents, trying to find the guy. "Sucks!" I complained like a child.

Just then Greg's phone chirped. He scrolled the text.

"Looks like Jeremy hooked up," Greg smiled.

"Eew. I didn't need to know that."

"Well, whatever. He says he's staying. She'll give him a ride home. Let's go," Greg said. He didn't have to tell me twice. I was back in the truck and ready to go. I felt so gross. All I could think about was how once I got my hands on that burrito, I'd be cured.

The ride down the mountain was bumpy and made us all

queasy. Leah grumbled and groaned from the backseat, and I held my forehead with my hand as if it would remedy the swirling pain in my brain. My mouth craved the bristly end of my toothbrush. Now, knowing that every time I went out I would feel like this the next day should have served as some sort of warning not to drink as much, or maybe not to drink at all, but it never stopped me from doing it the next time. In some cases, it didn't even stop me from doing it the very next night.

We got to the drive thru just in time. The three of us chowed down in the parking lot. I instantly felt better as the food hit my belly. Greg was fine, but he rarely got hangovers. I'm pretty sure that was a side effect of drinking every day. Come to think of it, I never saw him when he hadn't had at least one beer, and we never went a whole night without him having at least two or three more. Since he turned 21 he spent a lot of time with his buddies at the local bars. That's where all his money went. I'd venture to guess that most of his friends' money went toward his habit too, since he was always hitting people up for free drinks and cash. I know, he sounds like a total dud, but at the time, I didn't see it. I was in *love,* and I thought he was so *cool.*

Anyway, I was feeling better, and Greg was just dandy, but poor Leah wasn't quite so lucky. Greg drove us back to the street where I'd left my car. As soon as we got to my car, she had to throw up. Too bad it happened on a stranger's lawn. Luckily, the neighborhood wasn't really awake yet, so no one saw her; at least we don't think anyone did. It was kind of gross.

We drove back over to my house and crept in the back door. My parents knew where I spent the night, so we weren't being sneaky. We just didn't want to wake them up. It was nine a.m. on a Saturday, and my mom and dad liked to sleep in on weekends, since they had such early mornings during the week.

"Oh no," Leah said as she darted for the bathroom.

I shook my head, feeling lucky that I wasn't in the same position. I grabbed her a bath towel and some pjs and waited for her outside the door. I knew she'd need to take a shower to feel better. She opened the door and stuck a shaky hand out to grab the stuff.

"Thank you," she whispered.

I went to my room and sprawled out across my bed, clothes and all. I must have fallen asleep, because the next thing I knew, it was half past eleven, and my mom was knocking at the door to remind me I had to work. Thank goodness she remembered, because I certainly wouldn't have woken up without her telling me to. I hadn't set my alarm. I jumped up, showered, and got dressed as fast as I could. I told Leah to stay as long as she wanted, but she was barely awake. She threw her hand up in the air in acknowledgment and then passed out again. I grabbed my apron and my keys, and I ran out the door.

I arrived at work two minutes late.

"I'm sorry. I'm sorry. I'm sorry," I repeated as I rushed through the back door. I turned the corner to see who it was I was supposed to be relieving. It was Marnie. *Oh crap!* went through my head. The boss was glaring at me as I fussed with my apron.

"You know," Marnie said, "early is on time and on time is late, so you are..."

"I know. I'm so sorry," I apologized.

"It's okay. Good thing I was here to cover for you," she said passive aggressively. It was only two minutes. It wasn't as if she had to cover for me the whole day. I looked around. There was only one couple in the entire restaurant. They looked like they had just been seated. They were still scanning the menu. "So, they have drinks already. *I* got their drink order," she said, trying to emphasize her discontent that she had to get the drinks for the table.

"Where's Gail?" I looked around for the waitress that usually worked the shift before me.

"She had to leave a few minutes early. I actually called you this morning to see if you could come in earlier, but you never answered, so I had to come in," Marnie answered, scowling.

"Oh. I'm sorry. I didn't hear my phone," I apologized again. I felt like I was always apologizing for something when it came to Marnie. I had no idea she'd tried to call.

"It's fine, but I have somewhere to be, so you take it from here. I'll be back tonight to count out. Have a good day!" she said. She flashed a forced smile and waltzed out the back.

She had this way of making me feel incredibly guilty, and I was never exactly sure what I was supposed to be feeling guilty for. She had a real talent for it. I, of course, immediately checked my phone when she left. The battery was dead. I used the restaurant phone to check my messages. There was just the one message from Marnie. Her tone in the voicemail pissed me off. She insisted I call her back "as soon as possible" to confirm the "change in schedule", and if I couldn't get in there early, she would be "forced" to find another way to fill the gap between the shifts, which she didn't "want to have to do". *Forced*? Was it not *her* diner? If she hated being there so much, why did she own the place? And where was precious Ben? Poor thing was probably too hung over to get up. My guilt suddenly turned to inner rage, which was often the case when it came to Marnie. She'd blah blah blah me in this passive aggressive way about how terrible I was, I'd feel bad, and then I'd have a great epiphany that helped me see the situation as it was, but by that point, it was always too late to react the way I should have.

Work that day was quiet as usual. The couple had come and gone, and so had only a few others. It was nearing my third hour when I heard the oh so familiar jingle at the front door. I glanced up from the register and saw Leah dragging herself toward me.

"Somebody's looking better," I said sarcastically.

"Hardy har," Leah replied as she leaned herself sluggishly over the countertop. "I seriously feel like crap. How are you even alive?"

"Lucked out I guess. Did Bryan call you?"

"No. Not yet," she said, feeling her back pocket to make sure she had her phone on her.

"I thought you guys were supposed to go to dinner or something."

"Yeah, well, it's still early. He has time. Besides, look at me. I'm not exactly in the best shape," Leah grumbled.

"Well you better get with it fast because you really don't wanna screw this up. He's legit. You guys could really be something."

"Yeah? You think?"

"Heck yeah!" I encouraged. "He's hot, and he's got his stuff together, and he really likes you. This could be really good for you."

"Yeah. He is pretty great." A huge smile spread across her face. I could see the fantasy of the white dress and wedding cake dance through her head.

"So, what are you gonna wear?"

"Ugh!" she said painfully. "I haven't even thought about it. I have to go. I have to figure this out!" She'd made a complete turnaround. She went from hung over slug to giddy, first date girl in a matter of seconds.

"Good luck! Call me!" I called out as she skipped through the door.

I shook my head and smiled as I watched her pass by the large front window. She was grinning and shuffling along. She was excited, and I was excited for her. Leah needed someone to treat her well and take her out on dates. She needed something deeper than the one nighters she'd become known for. It looked like she finally had a chance at something solid.

The day came and went. There weren't many customers. I was tired from the night before, so I was glad that I wasn't busy, but feeling the ultra-thin wad in my right front apron pocket was a little disappointing. I'd only made twelve dollars in tips.

Stacey had called out sick again, and Ben would have been her alternate, except he didn't want to come in. Apparently, the night before had gotten him too. He called every twenty minutes to see if it was picking up, and when I'd tell him it was slow, he'd say, "well call me if it gets busy." Right. As if I would have time to call him if I were suddenly slammed with a restaurant full of people. I hated when he did that. Granted, I would rather he stay home and I not have to see him, but he was always shirking his responsibilities, and it drove me nuts. If he were at work, and I was the one calling in every so often to see if I *had* to come in, he certainly wouldn't stand for it.

Luckily, when Marnie came back in to close, she was in a more jovial mood. She didn't mention anything more in regards to my tardiness. The closing duties went smoothly, and I was free once again.

As I walked through the backdoor, I was met by a cool fresh breeze. It refreshed me after the long, stale day. I got in my car and immediately reached for my phone charger. I hooked my phone to it, and the charge light came on, a sign of revival. I turned it on and waited for the silly music and cartoon graphics to dance around. Finally, my menu came up. My phone started chirping immediately. I had eight text messages from Leah, and one vague and sort of unsettling text from Greg.

Leah's texts informed me that Bryan never called her. She had grown impatient and tried calling him around eight, but it went to his voicemail. She called him a slew of vulgarities and ended with a *Y AREN'T U RESPONDING! I NEED U! COME OVER AFTER WORK!* I clicked her a text back, apologizing for my phone dying and told her I'd be right over.

I then needed to respond to Greg. His text read: *WE*

HAVE 2 TALK. This seemed more like a phone call was in order, not a text message. I flipped through my call list and dialed Greg. His phone rang twice, then voicemail. Two rings and the outgoing message usually means someone is pressing IGNORE on their phone. After the tone, I spoke.

"Hey, babe. It's me. Sorry my phone died so I didn't get your text 'til just now. Anyway, I hope everything's okay. Give me a call when you get this. Love you."

I had a sinking feeling in my stomach, and I couldn't let it go without trying again, so I redialed Greg. This time one ring and the voicemail. I didn't leave a second message. I took in a deep breath and backed myself out of my spot and drove out through the alley. I knew the task at hand was emotional damage control for my best friend, but I couldn't help but worry about what Greg wanted to talk about. I convinced myself it was nothing. After all, he and I rarely fought, and things were really great between us.

CHAPTER TWO

As I pulled up to Leah's house, I tried to talk myself out of it, but I just had to try calling Greg one more time. This time, it went direct to voicemail. His phone was off. It was really gnawing at me, but I couldn't do anything about it at the moment, so I got out and prepared myself for the teary mess I was sure to find Leah in.

She already had the door open when I got to it.

"Come on," she said, leading me back to her room.

Becca was sitting on her bed, holding a tub of ice cream with two spoons.

"Want me to get you a spoon?" Becca asked.

"No, thanks," I said, shutting the door behind me.

Ice cream was their go to, feel better fast medicine. For me, it was just a stomach ache in a tub.

"So," I said, sitting next to Leah and Becca on Becca's bed, "have you heard from him?"

"No! Jerk." Leah had obviously been crying before I got there. She was all red and puffy. "And it's not like it should be a big deal or anything. I just feel so stupid."

"Maybe something happened to him. Have you tried calling him again? I'm sure he has a really good reason," I consoled.

"Yeah? I don't know. I don't want to call him again and

look all desperate."

"Yeah, but it's not really desperate since you guys *did* have plans. Just call him, and if he's weird about it, just say you wanted to make sure he's okay because you had plans," I suggested. "Or text him! That's more nonchalant."

"Yeah. Okay. Give me my phone," Leah ordered Becca.

Becca complied and handed her sister the cell phone. Leah tapped away at the keys.

"Okay," she said, "how does this sound? *Just want to make sure everything's ok. If you can't tonight, maybe some other time. Hit me up.*"

"Hit me up?" I asked, thinking that might be a little too nonchalant and just-one-of-the-guys-ish.

"Yeah. Well, that way he doesn't think I'm like pining over him or whatever, and it's casual, you know?"

"But, you don't want it to be casual," I pointed out.

"Right, but I don't want *him* to know that."

Oh the games people play when dating.

"Alright, well, it sounds good to me," I fibbed.

"Okay," Leah said. "Sent."

We sat in silence for a moment, staring at her phone. The backlight flashed off. Then a clicking sound came, and the light was back on. One new text message. We all jumped a little in anticipation.

She scrolled to the message. Her face scrunched up as she read. Her eyes filled up again.

"What does it say?" Becca prodded.

"*Sorry. My bad. I don't think this is going to work out. I'm looking for something more serious. Take care.*" The tears rolled down as she read aloud.

"What? What does that mean?" Becca asked.

"It means he doesn't want to date me because he heard I'm a slut," Leah sobbed.

"No," I said, knowing I was wrong. He shouldn't have put it so bluntly, and he shouldn't have judged her so easily, but sometimes one's reputation really does precede them. He should have at least come up with a tactful excuse. "He's just a jerk looking for a way out. He's probably still all butt hurt over Gina, and he just needs to get over himself. Forget him. There are plenty of other guys out there."

"Yeah, right." Leah blew her nose into a tissue.

"More ice cream?" Becca offered.

"No. I just need a minute," Leah said.

"Oh! I know what will make you feel better! I totally forgot!" Becca exclaimed.

"What?" Leah blubbered.

"I taped Brick Party Sundae's new video today! It's amazing. Brick has never been so hot." Becca ran toward the VCR. They had a small TV/VCR combo in their room. She flipped the TV on and rewound the video. "And here we go," she said gleefully as she leapt back to us on the bed.

We all watched in wonder as the video began. Nothing like a little BPS to brighten the day. The credits appeared in the bottom left hand corner. It was for their latest single "Weekend Riot". The band appeared on the screen in a house party setting. The party was going crazy because these famous band mates had just crashed their party. Brick's shirt was open, showing off his ridiculous abs. I was mesmerized by him. His gorgeous blue eyes were lined with eyeliner and his hair was dyed jet black with a blue streak down the right side. Now, this isn't a look I would usually go for on a man, but this man in particular was the most beautiful man I had ever seen. His chiseled body, his angular face, his angelic eyes, his perfect skin, and his soul piercing voice, made him the ultimate. He was like an unworldly creature. My whole body felt numb watching him. I almost forgot to breath as I soaked in every movement he made and every word he sang. When the camera flashed to the party people, or the other band members, I would almost get angry waiting for it to come back to Brick. I couldn't get enough of his face; I felt like when the camera was away from him, I might be missing something.

Yes, this all sounds crazy and obsessive, but it was Brick Donovan! He was pure perfection.

As the credits came back up on the bottom, left hand corner, we all exhaled a long, satisfied breath. The video was incredible. We'd all gotten our Brick fix.

"So," Becca broke the silence. "Feel better?"

"Well, Bryan is no Brick, now is he?" Leah responded. We all laughed. Leah was definitely almost back to her own. "Let's watch it again!" she insisted.

We ended up watching the video four more times. Every time felt like the first time. Brick was so charismatic; the television seemed made just for him. I called my mom to tell her I'd be staying over at Leah's. The three of us stayed up until three in the morning, eating junk food, playing with our hair, and gossiping. Sleepovers were just as fun as they were when we were kids. Greg never did call me back, but I put it out of my head. Most importantly, Leah was able to get her mind off Bryan, and we had a good night.

The next morning, I tried calling Greg again. I was semi surprised when he actually answered.

"Hello," he said in a groggy voice.

"Good morning, babe. Are you sleeping?" I asked, trying to be polite even though I was pretty miffed that he never called me back the night before.

"Yeah, but it's cool."

"So, what did you want to talk about?" I asked him.

"Uh... right, that. We can talk later," he said. He sounded wrecked.

"What did you do last night?" I inquired.

"I went to out," Greg answered curtly.

"Oh." I was surprised. I wasn't privy to the knowledge that he'd be going out partying. He usually told me when he had plans that didn't include me. "Where did you go?"

"Mulligan's." He was being really short and cold.

"Okay... did you have a good time?" I was trying my best not to sound weird or jealous. I was actually proud of myself. I sounded like I genuinely hoped he had a good time, rather than asking with a hidden meaning.

"Yeah. I did. Look, can we talk later? I gotta go," he said, cutting me off.

"Alright. That's fine." It wasn't fine, but it didn't look like I had an option.

"Okay, bye," he said.

"Bye. Love you," I answered, but he was already gone. He hung up before I could say goodbye. I said "Love you" to dead air.

This behavior was uncharacteristic to say the very least. He'd never gotten off the phone before without an *I love you*, and he'd never acted so indifferent. I searched my brain for things he could possibly be mad at me for, but nothing came to mind. It plagued me all the rest of the day. I didn't have to work, which was, for once, unfortunate, because I could have used the distraction. Leah agreed to hang with me all day. We decided to have Scary Movie Marathon Monday, and we rented some DVDs from the local video store and took them back to my place, where we ordered pizza and vegged out. My parents were at work, so we took advantage of the free living room.

Leah and I loved horror movies. We loved B movies especially; they seemed to be the most entertaining. We enjoyed poking fun at the laughable scenarios. Even though some of them seemed ridiculous and unrealistic, we always ended up scaring ourselves.

Potential Greg drama aside, it was a fun day. Leah lamented a little more over Bryan, but she had decided to officially let it go by the second movie. I explained Greg's weirdness, which she, being a good friend, told me was nothing to worry about. A couple pounds heavier, and three slasher movies later, we were over the boy madness, that is until my phone started chirping. I checked my texts, and there was a new message from Greg.

IM OUTSIDE. COME C ME, it read.

"Greg's outside. I'm just gonna go out for a few minutes. He wants to talk about something," I told Leah.

"Want me to pause this?" she asked. We were fifteen minutes into horror tape number four.

"No, thanks. I'll just be a minute."

I got up and made my way outside. There was a lump in my stomach where my nerves were setting up camp. The suspense had been killing me. He had been so weird, and I had no clue what he wanted to talk about. I was hoping for some grand romantic surprise. Maybe he was being short to hide some super sweet secret gesture he'd been planning. When I got to his truck, I could tell I was wrong. His face was solemn.

"Hey," I said, "what's wrong, babe?"

"Get in," he responded.

I pulled myself up into the passenger seat. We sat for a second in silence. I went to grab his hand, and he pulled away. This wasn't good.

"L, you know I love you, right?" he started.

"Yeah, of course."

"Okay, so what I'm about to tell you is not meant to hurt you or make you feel bad, okay?"

"Okay..." I said wearily.

"So, we've been together for like forever," he went on. Apparently *forever* was the equivalent of two years in his world. "If we keep going the way we're going, we'll get married, and that's, you know, great and all, but I just..." he trailed off.

"You just what?" I asked, getting a little angry.

"I just don't think I'm strong enough to not explore other options," Greg stated.

"Explore other options? What? Girls? You're not *strong enough* to not cheat on me? Is that what you're saying?"

"Well, yeah. I mean, I'm not saying there's someone else. I just think maybe we should take a little break to see what else is out there before we continue."

46

"Hold on," I interrupted, "you want to take a break from us so you don't have to feel guilty about sleeping with other chicks. Is that right?"

"Look, L, I'm just not sure if I can handle the idea that you'll be the last person I sleep with for the rest of my life. I'm young. It's hard to imagine right now. Believe me, this hurts me so much to have to do this," he said.

"Then why are you doing it?" I demanded. "This doesn't make any sense. If you love me, this wouldn't be happening."

"No, I do love you. That's why I have to do this. I need some time to make sure this is what I want, and I don't want to hurt you if something happens."

"Yeah, okay. If something happens? What does that mean? Did you hookup last night? Who is she?" My face felt like it was on fire. There were tears behind my eyes, but I was too angry to let them out.

"No, no, I swear. Nothing's happened... yet." His voice cracked and his mouth twitched in the upper right hand corner, the way it always did when he was lying.

"Yet? That's great, Greg. Well, I'm not so sure that you're the last guy I want to have sex with either, so this is terrific. But I can tell you this, when you're done doing all your *soul searching,* and *making sure*, or whatever the hell it is you think you need to do, I won't be here when you get back."

I threw open the door. I felt my feet hit the gravel in the driveway. My shoes felt heavy; my whole body felt heavy. I slammed the truck door and stormed off toward the house. A mess of thoughts filled my head. I was hurt, I was angry, I was sad, I was confused, and most of all, I was shocked. I felt betrayed. This person I had invested so much time in, a person I gave my entire heart to, just ripped me in half and didn't even bat an eye doing it. The tears finally found their way, and I couldn't keep them from pouring down my face. My first thought was *thank God I didn't let him see me cry.* He didn't deserve the satisfaction. I knew he was still there, parked in the driveway, but I didn't look back. I got safely inside the house. I propped myself up against the front door and waited for the sound of his truck driving away.

"God, L. What happened?" Leah was to her feet and right by my side.

I couldn't talk; I couldn't even breathe. I was crying so hard, I couldn't quite get the air in, and then, I needed to throw up. I ran past Leah and to the bathroom. After a few minutes in there alone, I stood at the sink and tried to talk myself down. I was almost more angry at myself than I was at him for letting him do this to me. I'd always thought of myself as strong and independent, and there I was, a blubbery, snotty mess because some boy dumped me. Looking back, I don't know what I saw in him that was really worth investing my heart. I guess we've all been there, but no matter how horrible the person is in hindsight, in the moment, a breakup feels like torture, unless maybe you're the one who gets to do the torturing.

Once I pulled myself together, I came to a realization. I needed a cigarette. A long time out with some nicotine sounded like a brilliant plan. I didn't smoke often, but this sure seemed like an appropriate time.

Leah was more than happy to accompany me out to the back yard. Whenever I smoked, I never wanted anyone to drive by and see me doing it, so I always retreated to the back yard. We sat, side by side, in matching plastic chairs and inhaled our nicotine in silence. Leah knew better than to press me for details when I was like this, so she patiently waited next to me until I was ready to talk.

After a few minutes of sitting, I was finally able to stop my lip from quivering long enough to tell her what happened. She, of course, was in full best friend mode, making all kinds of threats toward Greg and calling him all kinds of disgusting names to make me feel better. Her theatrical display actually did help. By the third time she mentioned kicking him in the balls, complete with an example of how she'd do it, I was smiling. She was pretty comedic when she needed to be, and sometimes by accident.

I didn't really feel better about the breakup, or about how he did it, but I did feel like a human again. I went in and out of this for the next few days. Needless to say I listened to Brick Party Sundae's *Love Meets Love* album over a dozen times that week. Some moments I would be fine and think I had come to terms with it, other moments I was crying hysterically; and a few times I found myself so angry, I wanted to kick him myself. Not once though did I allow myself to pick up the phone and try to contact him. That temptation lingered. Having had time to reflect on what happened, I of course came up with all sorts of clever things I should have said when he was breaking up with me. I had a whole new conversation worked out in my head, and I sounded like a mature woman capable of moving forward with not so much as a second thought. It was beautiful, and I really really wanted to recite it to him, but I chose not to go there. In reality, whenever someone tries to "make things better" by revisiting an old argument or telling the other they could care less, it really makes it seem like they care more. The last thing I wanted was to let him know that I was obsessing over this. I didn't want him to have the satisfaction. To ensure I never contacted him again, I of course made the very grown up decision of tagging a little reminder in my contact list. Instead of being listed as *Greg <3,* he was now listed as *Jackass - Do Not Call.*

I know guys like Greg aren't worth the all-consuming pain and sadness, but he was my first love, and it felt like someone had ripped my heart out and run me over with a dump truck. Going to work that week became even more of a chore. I was never in the mood for work, but I especially wasn't in the right frame of mind the first few days after Greg had torn out my insides and ran them through a juicer.

My body felt heavy from the emotional weight and empty from the lack of food. I could barely eat. My head was full of pressure from all the time I spent crying. I didn't bother with makeup, so I'm sure I looked about as great as I felt, but I really didn't care.

By that Friday, I looked a real mess. I was half way through my shift, when lo and behold, Ben waltzed in. Apparently, Stacey had quit, and Ben was now going to be there with me a lot more often. This was almost more depressing than my recent heartbreak.

"Wow," Ben said as he rounded the corner. "You look like ass."

"Aw," I replied, "thank you. That's so sweet."

"So what's up?" he asked.

"Nothing. Don't worry about it," I snipped.

"Does this have anything to do with Cheryl?"

Cheryl was a girl who had graduated a few classes ahead of mine. She was a twenty-one year old, mousy little thing with a bad attitude, who, though unattractive and relatively unpleasant to be around, did muster quite a bit of attention in recent months since she'd kind of turned herself into a party favor. She was known for random hookups, though no one ever really knew who with since the guys she slept with never wanted to brag about their nights with her. She was what they called a down low girl. Guys would hook up with her and then keep it on the down low. Disgusting, I know, but it was her choice.

"What about her?" I asked, though I would soon wish I hadn't.

"Cheryl and Greg are like a thing. They've been hooking up since Mulligan's."

"What?" The news didn't sound real. I repeated it in my head, but it didn't make sense. She wasn't pretty, and she was way too easy for my Greg to want to have anything to do with her. Then it hit me. She was actually perfect for Greg. This is what he said he wanted, so I guess he was really out there doing it. Then the word *Mulligan's* repeated in my head.

"Wait," I continued, "did you say Mulligan's?"

"Yeah, they hooked up last week at Mulligan's. They made out in front of everybody, and then they left for the parking lot, and well, you know. I mean, I didn't actually see the parking lot business, but everyone's saying it definitely happened." Ben had a creepy, self-satisfied smile on his face. He loved spreading gossip, and even more, he loved being the bearer of bad news.

There it was. I figured he'd cheated on me, but I didn't know for sure until now. The idea of him cheating was as bad as the idea that it was with Cheryl. The image of the two of them flashed in my head. It was disgusting. All of a sudden, my pride had taken a super hit. I felt a new pain on top of the pain that was already in my stomach. If a guy is going to cheat, shouldn't it be with someone more attractive or better than you? What did this say about me? Clearly, it didn't reflect on me being less adequate so much as it was a reflection on Greg being a total moron, but it still raised the question, and it still stung. Besides, what kind of guy was he that he makes out with the down low chick in public? I didn't blame her. She probably didn't know we were still together, or maybe she did; I don't know, but still, I blamed him for all of it.

My face twisted as the image of Greg and Cheryl together invaded my mind. Ben smiled, as if pleased by my discomfort. The more I thought about it, though, the clearer it became. This was actually a good thing. I knew the whole truth about who Greg was, and I really didn't want to be with someone like that. I suppose this realization usually takes longer, but for me, it was fairly instant. It was like the world shifted.

All of a sudden, the "maybe it's me's" or the "maybe I could have done something differently's" faded into the background. I no longer felt the desire to give him my grown up "I don't care about you" speech, because I actually didn't care. He was despicable, and I never wanted to see his lying, cheating face again. I didn't feel like crying anymore, which was strange. I felt relief. I was still mourning the loss of my wasted time, but I was no longer sad over Greg. I should have been angry. I should have been crazy with rage; I'm sure that's what Ben was expecting he would have provoked out of me, but it just wasn't there. His smile faded as my face untwisted with my newfound peace. I was free, and I was hungry.

"Well," I finally said after exploring my brain for the appropriate response, "thanks for telling me."

"Uh," Ben said, stunned by my nonchalant reaction, "sure. No prob."

I walked over to the pass thru window and ordered a turkey club. It was the tastiest sandwich I'd ever eaten. My stomach welcomed the food. The plate was soon clear, and I felt so much better.

The rest of the day went fairly routinely. I did all the side work and took most of the tables, as per usual, and Ben sat in the corner playing with his cell phone, as per usual. I didn't pay him much attention. I'd had enough anger filling me up in the last week to last a lifetime. I did get a little frustrated, however, when Marnie asked me to give Ben a ride home after work. His car was in the shop, and since she had dropped him off for his shift that day, and he couldn't possibly stick around an extra half hour to wait for his mommy to finish up, I of course got stuck driving him home. Apparently "waitress" also meant "chauffer".

That major inconvenience aside, at least my heartache had been dulled. That night I slept soundly for the first time in days. It was incredible.

CHAPTER THREE

Almost a month had passed since the demise of my relationship. My summer had quickly turned into a snore fest. When I wasn't working, Leah and I spent our time sunbathing and watching movies. We had some good times, laying out and gossiping, but there was something missing. Excitement. We hadn't partied or gone out in weeks. It was stifling hot though, so our ambition was at an all-time low.

Greg had disappeared from my mind almost altogether, and though I was definitely over the breakup, I was still completely miserable, with work that is. Seeing Ben almost every day, and working twice as hard to pick up his slack, was gnawing at me. I daydreamed constantly about quitting in some super inspired and all empowering way. I wanted to tell him and his mother exactly what I thought of them and that stupid place, but so far, it was just a fantasy.

It was a sticky hot day, and the air conditioner was busted in the restaurant. Most of the patrons came and didn't even bother getting seated. They were right back out the door. Summertime is way too hot in Farber. People go to restaurants and the movies and the shopping mall to escape the heat, not embrace it. A few people were brave enough to sit at the table outside, but for the most part, the broken air conditioner had ruined business that day.

Leah waltzed in through the front door around four and giddily skipped up to the counter, where she took a seat.

"Dude!" she yelled. "It's flippin' hot in here!"

"I know!" I agreed.

"Well, hello there, Leah," Ben said as he slinked around the corner. He was carrying a bucket of ice from the back to fill the ice bin.

"Satan," Leah acknowledged Ben.

"Need a cool down?" he asked her, nodding toward his bucket.

"No, thanks. The image of you coming anywhere near me with that bucket is already giving me the shivers, and not in a good way," Leah zinged.

"Ouch. Well, if you change your mind, I'll be out back." Ben pulled a cigarette from his pocket and placed it in his mouth, winking at my friend. Then, luckily, he was out the back door.

"Ugh, I hate that guy," Leah said, stealing the thought from my head. "Anyway... check this out!" She pulled a clipping from a magazine out of her pocket. "Read it!" She handed it to me.

"No way!" I said as I read the ad. "They're gonna be so close!"

Brick Party Sundae was adding new dates to their tour, and they were going to be doing nine extra shows in Texas; the first show was the very next week in Hadley, only two hours away from Farber.

"I know, right!" Leah squealed. "We have to go!"

"I wish. Leah, the tickets are probably like a million dollars."

"L, I looked it up, and we can get crap seats for like twenty bucks. Come on! We have to go!" Leah's eyes were glazed over with excitement.

"Yeah, okay. Hadley's only a couple hours. I can probably get the night off."

"That's the spirit, L!" Leah shouted. "But I was thinking,

and you know what would be really cool?"

Uh oh, there was a plan brewing, a serious plan. I could always tell when Leah wanted to get us into trouble; it always started with, *you know what would be really cool?* or *I have the best idea!* Those two phrases always meant something kind of huge was playing out in her mind.

"No, I don't want to know," I jested.

"Yes, you do. Trust me."

Trust me. Another phrase that always accompanied a crazy Leah scheme.

"So here's what I'm thinking," Leah went on, "we go to all of them!"

"All of what?" I asked.

"All the shows! We follow BPS around Texas!" She smiled wide, so proud of her ridiculous proposal.

"You're nuts!" I laughed at her. "We can't do that."

"What? Why not?"

"Well," I explained, not really sure why I had to state the obvious, "for one, we don't have the kind of money it takes to go chasing tour buses. Plus, I have to work. Oh, and you seem to be forgetting, early enrollment is in a few weeks. The last tour date on here is the night before enrollment."

"Okay, buzz kill, I actually did think about all that. First, we have money. I have a few hundred saved up from babysitting and grad gifts, and you have that little fund in the bank."

"Leah, that little fund is for my tuition."

"Yeah, yeah, I know," she replied, "but, we don't have to use much. We can do this on the cheap."

"Leah," I said sternly, "gas, concert tickets, hotels, nothing on that list is going to be cheap."

"L!" She was not giving up. "We'll split the gas, we don't have to stay in hotels, we can camp or sleep in the car, and tickets are not an issue. We can hang out before the concerts and buy from scalpers for like next to nothing."

"For one thing, two girls in the middle of nowhere,

sleeping in a car sounds like the opening for a horror flick, and for another, scalping is illegal!"

"Okay, fine, we'll find flea bag places we can afford, and we'll just eat gas station food. B T Dub, the legalities of scalping is the scalpers problem, not the buyer's."

"Yes it is! People who buy the tickets are arrested just as often," I pointed out. I wasn't actually one hundred percent on that, but I had seen a story line like that on a TV show once. This guy bought a scalped ticket and the scalper was a cop, or something like that.

"Ugh! God, L, you're being so lame. This is gonna be the adventure of a lifetime! Besides, you hate your job. You need a vacay. Aside from this nasty place, there's nothing keeping you here. Wouldn't you like to get out of here for a minute? On the open road, no worries. Leave all the boy drama and small town crap behind for a while? We haven't done jack all summer. School starts in like a month. I mean, it's Brick Party Sundae! It's Brick Donovan!"

She made a compelling argument. I did want to get away; I did hate my job; and I really did love Brick and BPS.

"What about enrollment?" I asked Leah. I didn't want to miss out on the classes I wanted.

"We'll skip the last date and come home. Promise," Leah said, eyes on fire.

"Uh." I still wasn't sold. I had too much responsibility guilt. I couldn't just up and leave my job for three weeks. If we were super careful with our money, it did seem feasible that we could budget this adventure without totally screwing me up for tuition, but I was still uneasy about it. "I'll think about it. But we're definitely going to the Hadley show."

"Yes! Awesome. We'll talk later. I'm totally gonna get you on board. This is gonna be the best summer of our lives!" Leah cheered. "But I have to go. I am dying in here. This heat is gross. Love ya! L Squared!" she shouted.

"L Squared!" I yelled back. She skipped back out the front, the bells jingling behind her.

I shook my head as I tossed the idea around. It sounded amazing, but completely irresponsible. Then again, isn't this the kind of thing people are supposed to do at eighteen? I mentally added up the figures. I started to imagine that we could probably pull it off for just a few hundred dollars. Since the beginning of summer, I hadn't really done much spending, plus a few "congratulations on your graduation" cards had rolled in with checks inside, and I was up to almost seven hundred in my bank account. I'd already made my car payment for the month, so the rest was pretty much icing. I tallied up the potential cost of classes; twenty dollars per unit for twelve units put me at two hundred forty for tuition, and then there were books, which I figured wouldn't be much if I stuck to the used ones. I decided that with all that, and if I didn't buy the back to school wardrobe I was planning on, I could actually swing it. We'd each have a few hundred to go on the road with. We might really be able to make it happen.

Then my mind flashed to my parents. I wasn't really sure how they'd feel about me gallivanting all across the state, chasing a rock band. Then my mind flashed to Brick Donovan. I imagined what might happen if, during one of his songs, he pulled me up on stage, and we fell in love right then and there. We'd get married and travel the world together, sharing his beautiful voice with the masses. How could I pass up the chance? It wasn't likely that something like that would happen, but it was a really fun thought to entertain.

Just as I was naming my and Brick's unborn children, the phone rang.

"Miss Marnie's," I answered cheerily.

"Did the A/C guy call back yet?" Marnie's voice asked through the receiver. No greeting, just a question.

"No. No phone calls at all actually," I replied.

"Okay, well, I need you to call him and see when he's going to make it in there. I would, but I don't have the number on me. His card's in the rolodex under Ace Air."

Bark, bark. No *please*; no *thank you*. Not shocking, just annoying. "Call me back when you know."

"Alright, I'll try him now."

"Okay. Bye." Then she hung up.

Great. She wasn't even nice about it. I was sick of getting bossed around. Yes, I know, she was my boss, so technically bossing was her prerogative, but that didn't mean she had to be such a raging beast all the time. She could have looked up the number in the phone book, called 411, or even asked me for the number from the rolodex, but no, I had to do it. I had to call the guy. I didn't realize "waitress" not only meant "chauffer" but also meant "secretary".

I dialed the number for Ace Air and let the phone ring several times in my ear before giving up. I hit redial and let it ring ten more times before I decided to hang up again. There wasn't an answering machine. I knew, though, if I didn't try at least once more, Marnie wouldn't be satisfied, so I dialed, this time without redial, in case my first dial was incorrect, and the phone just rang on as it had before. Feeling defeated, I picked up the receiver to call Marnie back.

"Yeah," she answered sourly. I wondered, did she have caller id or did she answer the phone like an unpleasant troll for every caller?

"Hey, it's L. I tried three times, and no one is picking up over there. Sorry," I apologized.

"Are you sure you called the right number?" she challenged.

"Yeah. I called the number off the card in the rolodex. No one answered."

"Did you leave a message?" she asked.

"No. They didn't have a machine."

"They didn't have a machine? What kind of business doesn't have a machine?" She was clearly displeased.

"Well, maybe theirs isn't working, or they're on the other line or something. I don't know. I can try later," I offered.

"No. Give me the number. I'll try them myself," Marnie

snorted. This is what she should have done in the first place, but I wasn't going to tell her that and ruffle her feathers even more. I gave her the telephone number, repeating it twice so that she couldn't call back and say I gave her the wrong info.

Again, no *thank you*, just a click, and she was gone. A few minutes later, the phone was ringing again.

"Miss Marnie's," I answered.

"What kind of business doesn't have an answering machine?" Marnie's voice complained. I guess she'd found out for herself that what I had told her was accurate. She couldn't possibly take my word for it.

"I guess they're not open. So no one's coming in today to fix the A/C?" I asked.

"Well if I can't get someone on the phone, I doubt anyone will be coming in there." A simple no would have sufficed, but she of course had to make me feel stupid for asking.

"Well, that's too bad," I said politely. "It's really hot in here. There isn't much business today."

"Well, I don't see a point then in there being two of you on for the dinner shift," she reasoned. My ears perked up. She was actually going to let me go home early. "Go ahead and tell Ben he can go. I'll be in around nine to close up."

Ben? Tell Ben he can go? NOOOOO!

"Okay," I said sheepishly. I wanted to scream how unfair it was that I had to sit and melt for an entire eight hours alone while Benny Boy only had to tough it out for one and a half.

"Oh," Marnie added, "before he goes, I need you to hop next door and pick up my dry cleaning. It's ready, but I can't get there before they close."

Apparently "waitress" now meant "chauffer", "secretary", and "errand girl".

"Well," I said, thinking logically, "Ben could probably just grab it on his way home. I'll let him know..."

"No," she cut me off. "He doesn't like going over there.

Just go get it and hang it up in the back for me."

He doesn't *like* going over there? So what?

"Okay," I said even though I wanted so badly to say something else. "Do you just want me to have him bring it home with him?" That seemed sensible.

"No. Just hang it up for me. He'll probably want to go do something. Okay, see you tonight." And she was gone again.

So I was now supposed to run her personal errands and let the boy wonder off the hook again. My face grew hot as the rage rose up inside me. I looked around at all the empty tables. Somehow all this extra nonsense and bullying didn't seem worth minimum wage and zero potential of tips. Granted, the air conditioning would likely be fixed in the next couple days, and business would pick back up, but I had finally had enough.

"Hey, loser face. Was that my mom on the phone?" Ben came around the corner and pulled my apron strings, untying them to be a pain.

Instead of tying the bow back together like I usually did when he childishly pulled it loose, I simply pulled the apron off.

"Yeah. It was. She said since business is slow, I can go home," I said. I watched his face sink as he heard the bad news. "So, you're on your own." I pulled my purse out from under the counter and got my keys out. "Oh," I continued, "you need to pick up her dry cleaning next door. And, wait, one other thing," I added as a final thought, "I quit. Buh-bye."

My adrenaline was pumping. My entire body was jittery with excitement and nerves. Walking out on my job was possibly the dumbest thing I'd ever done, but it was also the most liberating. I knew there was probably no going back. Once you made Marnie's crap list, you were on it for life. Going back inside and telling him I was joking had crossed my mind as I got in my car, but it only lasted a second. As soon as I turned the key in that ignition, I was out of there. No looking back. It felt incredible.

I turned up the volume on my car stereo. Brick Party Sundae blared through my speakers as I roared through town. I felt cool; I felt like I could do anything. Sitting at a red light, with BPS rattling through my car, I texted Leah with *I'm in!* :)

The light turned green, and the road opened up in front of me. Possibility and adventure paved the streets. I couldn't wait to embark on this great journey.

And then, I came to a great realization. *My parents are gonna be pissed.*

It was a little after five when I got home. My mom and dad were both already back from work.

"You're home early," my mom said as I walked in.

"Yeah, uh, I kind of quit today," I admitted.

"You quit? What are you talking about? Why?"

"Marnie. She's insane. She has me giving Ben rides around off the clock, picking up her laundry, and sitting in a hundred and twenty degree heat. I just can't stand it anymore, so I left." I looked at my mom with big puppy dog eyes, pleading for sympathy.

"Well," she said, "I hope you don't think this means you're going to be lazing around here the rest of the summer."

"No. Not exactly," I muttered.

"What's not exactly? Do you have something lined up?"

"Well, sort of." There was no avoiding it now. I had to tell her L Squared's plan for the greatest summer of all time. "Leah and I kind of made travel plans."

"Travel plans?" My mom tilted her head and looked at me sternly. "You quit your job so you can travel? Where? With what money?"

"No. I told you why I quit. It just so happens though that we have this plan."

"Oh great. L and Leah have a plan. I can't wait to hear

this," she noted sarcastically. "Hang on. Rick! Rick get in here!" she called to my father in the kitchen. "L wants to tell us of her exciting end of summer plans."

"Oh yeah? What's that L.L. Bean?" my dad asked as he appeared in the living room. Since I insisted on having everyone call me L, he always came up with the oddest little nicknames with L's in them. L.L. Bean was one of my personal favorites.

"Okay," I braved on, "Leah and I want to go to this concert."

"A concert?" My dad asked. "Well that doesn't sound so bad."

"Yeah, except it's more like eight concerts... in different cities... on different days, so we'd be gone for a while. But, don't worry, we'll never be more than ten hours away from home at all times."

"Are you insane?" my mom interjected. "You want to go follow some band all around Texas? Two girls, alone?"

"Well, yeah. But don't worry, we'll be totally careful, and it'll only be a couple weeks."

"A couple weeks? You want to drive all up and down the state for a couple weeks? How are you going to pay for this little adventure?" Mom probed.

She was trying to wear me down, make sure I had a solid plan. I knew the game, and I was prepared to play; I was prepared to win. I had to get out. I had to see Brick Donovan in the flesh. I needed to experience the open road.

"I have some savings, and we've figured it out, and we can make it work for next to nothing. Really. It won't cost much at all. I'll still have enough for tuition and stuff." I stretched the truth a tad. We hadn't figured it all out yet. Not even close, but I knew we would, and knowing we would was just as good in my mind as having already done it. At least, that was always my logic when it came to explaining stuff to my parents. Like when Mom would call up from work and ask if I'd taken out the trash, and I'd say yes when I really hadn't yet. The intention to do it was there, and it would get done eventually, so, therefore, it wasn't really a lie, right?

"I don't know, L. This sounds kind of nuts," she countered. She was starting to lean into the idea though. I could see it. And then she said the oh so transparent words, "what do you think, Rick?" Whenever she hadn't already said no, and she looked to my dad for his opinion, it always meant she was considering it. Now, it wasn't as if I really needed their permission, being eighteen and all, but I did live in their house, and I did respect their opinion, and as adult as I liked to think I was, I still needed them, and I still looked to them for their approval.

"Oh, Maggie, I don't know. This sounds dangerous. Do you think she's ready for something like this?" my dad asked my mom. This was also good. They were discussing the situation as if I weren't there, which meant they were actually entertaining the possibility.

"She has to get out there some time, I guess," my mom concluded. "What about school? Would you be back in time for early registration? You know if you miss it, then you can't register until the week classes start, and you won't get the courses you want."

"I know. Don't worry. We'll be back in plenty of time. We have it all worked out," I assured.

"What about sleeping? Where are you staying?" my dad asked.

"Well," I stalled as I thought. We really hadn't thought it through. I hadn't done any research at all. Camping was definitely out of the question as far as my parents were concerned; I knew that. Sleeping in the car would also be a no go. "We haven't booked anything yet, but Leah has found some discounted rates at some hotels. If we share a queen size bed, it's even cheaper. Plus, I have my auto club card. That's a discount right there, right?"

"Yeah, it is. Make sure you have that on you at all times

in case something happens with the car," my mom said.

Yes! Home free. She said to make sure I did something while I was on my trip, which meant she was okay with me going.

"I will. I promise," I said.

"Okay, well, we'll talk more about this later. I have to go figure something out for dinner. Oh, and you better have a plan for new employment when you get back from this little tour of Texas, alright?"

"Of course. I'll have a new job in no time."

I was sure it wouldn't be too difficult to get another job when I got back. I hadn't really thought about it yet, but I figured I'd be just fine. I hoped so anyway. Applying for jobs was the last thing on my mind at that moment. I was going on the road to follow Brick Party Sundae! Nothing seemed more important.

CHAPTER FOUR

Over the following week, Leah and I researched a bunch of hotels online and came up with a simple budget. We only booked a room for the one night we were spending in Hadley. We were sure we could get a room in the other cities no problem, and we'd heard that sometimes the rates drop at the last minute, so you could just show up and get a room in person. We also decided to purchase the first night's concert tickets online. Leah and I didn't want to take any chances on missing the first show.

We each raided our household pantries and grabbed a few things that might go unnoticed, like crackers and chips and stuff. It was a little easier at her house. With five other kids, it wasn't uncommon for the goldfish and fruit snacks to go missing rather quickly. I guess one could say this was kind of like stealing, but we justified it with the simple fact that if we were home, we'd be eating this stuff anyway, so it was more like hoarding and not sharing.

We had snacks in my car, full packs of cigarettes in our purses, almost our entire closets packed into bags, driving directions printed from the internet, and a tank full of gas. L Squared was ready to go.

The day had finally come. I say finally, but the week really did seem like an eternity since we were so excited. In the early morning, I hugged my parents, wished them both a great day at work, promised I'd call to check in often, and I was on my way.

I rolled up to Leah's house and texted that I was outside. Five minutes of waiting, I was getting a little worried that she'd missed her alarm. I tried calling. No answer. I was just about to get out of my car and go to the door when she came flying out of it. She ran up to the trunk and tapped it as a signal for me to open it. She put one last bag, which she hadn't already put in my car in the days before, into the trunk. She slammed it shut and ran around to the passenger side.

"Let's get outta here!" she yelled excitedly as she cozied into her seat.

"Done!" I responded, and we were off.

"It's the perfect day for a getaway," Leah said as we started off on our journey.

"It is indeed." I looked at her and laughed. "So, what did you end up telling your mom?"

Leah was apprehensive about telling her mom what she was going to be doing. Even though she was eighteen, her mom still tried to keep her under strict surveillance. I mean, she still had to lie to her when we were going to parties, so driving cross country, or cross Texas in our case, would have clearly been out of the question.

"Uh..." Leah hesitated. Obviously she hadn't chosen the truth route. "I sort of might have told her we were going camping... with your family."

"What? Are you crazy? What happens when your mom runs into my mom at the grocery store or something?"

"Well, let's just hope that doesn't happen." Leah giggled nervously.

"Yeah, let's hope," I added, shaking my head. "Put on some music!" I motioned toward the CD case on the floor board near her feet.

"What should we listen to?" she asked sarcastically. "I know! Brick Party Sundae!"

She pulled out one of the four BPS CDs from the case and slid it into the slot. She turned the volume knob to the right, and the first song blasted through the speakers. We both busted out in song, singing along to one of our favorite tunes. Brick's voice wafted over us, and luckily, drown out our own feeble attempts at singing his beautiful words. This was it; the start of our big adventure.

We sang along to the next three songs and then let the music play in the background as a soundtrack to our road trip. Two hours, a few pieces of red licorice, and a ton of giggles later, we were in Hadley, Texas. I called my mother to let her know we made it to Hadley safe and sound. I'd promised her I would call every single morning of the trip as well as every time we made it to a new stopover spot. She was at work so the conversation was fairly short.

Hadley was insanely hot. We couldn't check into our hotel until three, so we had to find something to do. Neither of us had ever spent much time in Hadley, so we decided to go exploring.

After driving around town for a few minutes, we spotted a cute coffee shop on the main street. We hadn't really figured coffee into our budget, but we thought, *why not?* It was after all, the first day of our adventure. We decided we should have a little treat.

As we entered the place, the aromas of freshly brewed coffee and just out of the oven pastry treats fell over us. It smelled heavenly. I was already looking forward to going there again the next day, and we hadn't even ordered yet.

We approached the register and found ourselves second in line. I looked over the gorgeous pastries and muffins in the glass case to the right of the register. I glanced quickly at the menu, placed high on the wall behind the girl at the register. They had a plethora of fancy drink combinations and coffee blends. I couldn't even pronounce half of them, but nevertheless, they sounded amazing. In this kind of heat, of course, something on ice was preferable.

The guy in front of us paid for his iced tea and moved away, leaving the space open to us.

"What can we get started for you?" the pretty barista asked with a big, friendly smile. Her name tag said *Bethany*. She had perfectly straight, sparkly white teeth. I couldn't help but smile back at her.

"I would like," I said slowly, glancing once more at the menu, "a sixteen ounce iced vanilla latte and one of those chocolate croissants, please." I pointed to the case.

"Sure," she said. "Are you two together?"

"Yeah," I said as I shuffled to the right to make room for my friend, "go ahead, Leah."

"Hi!" Leah greeted the girl. "I'd like the same coffee thingy as her and a blueberry scone."

"Alright. Will that be all for you ladies?" the girl asked.

I looked to Leah to make sure. She was still looking over the menu.

"Oh, yeah. Sorry," she finally said. "That's it."

"Okay," the barista continued, "that'll be thirteen twenty six."

I handed her a twenty and then put a dollar from the change she gave me into her tip jar.

"Thank you," she said. "We'll have those right out for you over there." She pointed to the designated pick-up area at the end of the counter. We walked over and stood, waiting for our treats.

As we waited, I noticed a good looking guy waltz in. A notebook page dangled in his hand. It looked like a list. My eyes quickly went to his arms. They were beautifully tanned and very toned. He was wearing a tight white t-shirt, that fit perfectly to his biceps, and olive green cargo pants. He had straight, medium length, shiny, brown hair. He swept a lock out of his face as he stepped up to the register.

The girl, Bethany, immediately noticed how gorgeous he was too. Her smile was even bigger than when we were ordering, and her cheeks turned red. He flashed her a sexy smile and made some chit chat that I couldn't hear. Then he handed her the notebook page. She nodded and started pushing buttons on the cash register. He handed her a large bill and put a ten in her tip jar. Not only was he extremely good looking, but he was generous. She thanked him, and he walked over to where we were standing. I nudged Leah, but I guess I didn't have to; she was already visually glued to him as well.

We both tried to look away so as not to be so obvious. He got closer, and I could smell his subtle and extremely sexy cologne.

"Good morning, ladies," he greeted us as he settled next to me.

I looked around for a second to make sure he was talking to us.

"Hi," I said, smiling at him. It was almost difficult to look right at him. His face was so perfect. It was sort of angular and perfectly chiseled. There was a shadowy outline where he obviously hadn't shaved yet that day. He had insanely blue eyes and thick, dark lashes that made them look even brighter. He looked strangely familiar, although I was sure I'd never met this guy before.

"I'm Blue," he said, putting his hand out to greet me.

"Like the color?" I said stupidly as my hand met his. I immediately regretted saying that, but it's what came out.

"Yeah, like the color," he said, laughing. He smiled a perfect smile. He almost didn't look real. He looked like one of those cartoon princes or one of those ridiculously good looking underwear models for fancy, designer underwear. "And you are?" he asked.

"I'm L," I said.

"Like the letter?" he asked.

"Yeah, like the letter," I replied. I felt like we had this amazing banter going. I was totally into it. I thought maybe he might have actually been flirting with me. "This is my friend, Leah."

"Hi, Leah. Blue. Nice to meet you." His hand now met hers.

"Nice to meet you," she said. She blushed a little.

"So," Blue went on, "you girls live here?"

"No," I answered, "we're in town for a concert."

"Ah, BPS fans, eh?" he asked.

"Two iced vanillas, scone, and croissant?" A voice came from behind the counter.

"That's us," Leah said to the guy who had filled our order. "Thanks," she added as she grabbed our stuff. She handed my cup and treat bag to me.

"Thanks," I said. "I'm sorry, what were you saying?" I turned back to Blue.

"I was asking if you two were fans of BPS," he reminded.

"Oh yeah," I said, "probably the biggest fans ever. We love them." I immediately regretted that too. I sounded like such a dork. I wanted to be cool and interesting, and I felt like I was sounding like a total nimrod.

"Cool," he said.

"Are you a fan?" Leah asked him.

"Yeah. I guess you could say that." He smiled a sideways grin.

"Order for Blue?" the man's voice cut in again.

"Right here." Blue put his hand up. "Well, that's me. I have to get these back. It was nice meeting you girls. Maybe I'll see you around." He went over to the pick-up and lifted the large box of coffees and treats that were carefully packed in.

"Nice to meet you, too," we both said, almost in unison. We laughed, waved, and watched him as he walked out the door.

I was disappointed that it was over. He was gone, and I would never see him again. I'd never talked to someone that gorgeous before, much less flirted with someone that gorgeous. It seemed like he was flirting anyway, or maybe that was just wishful thinking.

My eyes were fixed on the door.

"Hey, L!" Leah's fingers snapped in front of my face. She laughed as I turned back to her. "You wanna just sit here?"

"Yeah. Sure," I said.

We took a seat at a small table in the corner.

"Was that guy hot or what?" she asked, pounding her straw on the table to loosen the wrapper.

"Hot is not even the word for whatever he was," I answered, laughing.

"He was totally into you, L. You should've gotten his number."

"No way. He probably has a girlfriend, a really perfect one. Besides, we're only here for one night; then we're on to Stover." I took a drink of my latte. The flavor startled me. It was delicious. We didn't have coffee drinks like this in Farber. "Dude, we totally need one of these places in Farber," I shared.

"No kidding. This is so good. Bite?" She held her scone in front of my face.

"Yes, please. Here," I said, handing her a piece of my chocolate croissant.

"Oh! This is phenomenal!" Leah cooed through her teeth.

"Right?"

"We are so coming back tomorrow," Leah decided.

"Yes, yes we are." I agreed, tipping my cup in her direction.

We sat there for about twenty minutes, and then we decided to do some sightseeing. It had been a few years since either of us had been to Hadley, so we didn't really know where anything was. We drove around. The town was a lot smaller than we thought it was. It was larger than Farber, but it only took fifteen minutes for us to drive up and down the main drag and weave around some of the more business populated side streets. We spotted our hotel, but we were still too early to check in, so we decided to do some window shopping around the local stores. We walked up and down and all around for almost an hour.

Finally, Leah couldn't stand it anymore and had to buy something. We stood in front of a tiny little clothing store and stared at a shiny, sequin tank top in the window.

"That's really pretty," I said.

"Yeah. I have to have it," Leah announced.

"What? No. Clothes are not in our budget," I tried to remind her.

"Okay, but neither was coffee and we went to the coffee place, right? Besides, one little shirt isn't going to break the bank. I'll just be more thrifty tomorrow." She sounded serious, as if she actually could eliminate her spending for a day to make up for this purchase. Unfortunately, Leah could justify the crap out of anything in any given situation, and more often than not, she always fell short on the flip side of her bargains.

"Whatever. No caffeine heaven for you in the morning, I guess."

"Come on," she ordered, grabbing my hand and pulling me through the doors of the store.

As she tried on her must have top, I sorted through the racks, looking at all the beautiful clothes. A few things called out to me, but in the forefront of my mind was exactly how much money I had and exactly how I wasn't supposed to spend it.

"Cute, huh?" Leah called out from behind me.

I turned to see my friend twirling around in front of a large mirror, admiring her choice.

"Yeah, it's cute. How much is it?" I had to ask. I wasn't convinced by her little spend today be frugal tomorrow speech.

"Not a lot," she replied and then danced back to the dressing room to change out of it. *Not a lot* was definitely code for *I'm not going to tell you how much, because you'll talk me out of buying it*; if it was actually doable on our budget, she would have told me exactly what the price was. In reality, nothing extra was really doable on our budget. We weren't supposed to buy anything but gas, discount food, seedy shelter, and concert tickets.

She waltzed up to the register, sparkly shirt in hand, and eagerly grabbed for her wallet. I rolled my eyes at my friend's flippancy, but she didn't see it. If she had, she probably wouldn't have cared anyway. I crept up behind her to get an ear on whatever the sales girl said.

"Forty two ninety," the girl behind the register announced proudly, as if that were a bargain.

42.90! ricocheted in my head. That was more than her share for one night at a shabby shack hotel. It was actually only ten bucks shy of the total for our room in Hadley that night.

"Leah!" I scolded.

"What, L? It's no big. I said I'd make it up; I'll make it up," she reasoned.

"Yeah. Well looks like you're eating the stuff from the trunk for the rest of the trip, and I'm getting stuck with the gas."

"L, really. It's fine."

"Oh, for the love of Mike," I said under my breath.

"Who's Mike? Is he hot?" she asked, flipping her hair to the side as if she was off the hook.

"Cute. Real cute," I said, obviously annoyed.

"L, seriously. Calm down. It's really not that big a deal," she said again.

My head was shouting, *It's a huge deal! I can't believe you!* But my mouth never let the words out. There obviously was no talking her out of it, so I just shook my head and tried to let it go. I waited for her to finish up and grab her receipt for her overpriced shirt.

"Seriously though," she said as we walked out the door,

"who's this Mike?"

I couldn't help but laugh. She giggled with me, and we continued to walk around a bit longer.

Three finally rolled around, and we were able to check into our hotel, which actually turned out to be a motel. Our room was on the second floor, and we faced the main street. It was about what could be expected for fifty three dollars a night. Fifty three dollars sounds like a lot of money, but come to find out, hotels are insanely expensive. It was the cheapest we could find, and I was really hoping, actually counting on, the prices not being much more in the rest of the towns we were headed for.

The room was musty and smelled of stale cigarettes. We immediately opened the window, which had a safety stick inserted inside and only allowed the window to open about four inches. I turned on the air conditioner, which rattled loudly and only pushed out semi cool air. It was too hot to sit around in there, so we decided to take advantage of the fact that our motel had a pool.

We took the towels from our room down to the pool area, which turned out to be a smart plan of action as there weren't any towels poolside. We draped the towels over the faded green lounge chairs. The chairs were hot to the touch, and since the towels weren't very long, we strung our tops and shorts along them to make up the difference. I attempted flipping off my flops, but the concrete burned my feet. I glanced around for shade to move into, but there was none. The sun was so bright and hot, it was borderline abusive.

"Pool?" I asked Leah, looking at her squinting face. We had on sunglasses, but the sun was still trying to penetrate them. Lines from the heat rose from the ground.

"Yes!" she replied.

"Whatever you do," I warned, "do not take off your flip flops."

She laughed, and we shimmied over to the water. We were the only ones outside. I looked into the pool and inspected the water. It was pretty clean; a few leaves and a couple bugs but nothing of great concern.

We dropped our shoes by the edge on the shallow end and walked down the steps into the water. The water was almost shocking. It wasn't heated, by the sun or otherwise. It was cold. The transition wasn't easy. We wanted to cool down, but the water seemed ice cold. It may have seemed colder than it actually was since we were especially hot.

"Whoa! This water is freezing!" Leah squealed. We'd both only gotten in mid-thigh.

"I know!" I shrieked back. "Maybe if we just dive in."

"Yeah, okay," she said sarcastically, "after you."

"Together. Count of three," I suggested. She nodded, and I counted, "one, two, three!" I dunked my entire body under the water. It felt like a thousand icy pins against my shoulders and on my scalp. I held myself under for a few seconds. Soon, the water felt amazing. I popped back up and felt rejuvenated and refreshed. I was glad I did it. "Woo!" I called out. I wiped the water from my eyes and looked over to see a completely dry Leah.

"Hey!" I shouted. "No fair! You jerk!" I laughed and splashed water toward her. She squealed and moved away.

"Sorry. Okay, I'm going," she said, looking down toward the bottom of the pool. "I'm gonna do it," she said. She took in a deep breath and closed her eyes. She went to dip down and then jumped instead. "I can't do it. No, I can." She was trying hard to psych herself up for the plunge.

"Dude, it's not that bad," I assured her. "Just do it, you chicken."

"Okay, okay. I'm going. I'm going. No really, I'm going." She hesitated.

"Just go!" I said impatiently.

She took in a deep breath and dropped herself into the water. She popped back up, laughing and screeching.

"Ah!" she yelled, "that's flippin' cold!"

We laughed. Both of us, now used to the temperature,

paddled around for a few minutes and then took a crouched position at the four foot mark.

"Hey," Leah said, "I forgot to tell you something. I got you a present."

"A present?" I was instantly intrigued.

"Yep. I got us some identification." Her right eyebrow went up dubiously.

"Identification? What like passports and social security cards? Are we on the lam?" I asked, laughing.

"No." She splashed water at me. "I got us some IDs. We are officially legal. To drink I mean."

"No way! Where did you get fake IDs?"

"They're not fake. They're just not ours," she informed me, winking. "Your name is Melissa Scholl, and you are from Mississippi."

"Wait, what?" Confusion replaced my intrigue.

"They're real IDs, but they once belonged to other people. I swear they look just like us though. No one would be able to tell the difference. Just memorize whatever info is on it in case someone questions you."

"If they look just like us, why do I need to memorize anything?" The whole idea sounded crazy.

"Just in case. It'll be fine. They're totally legit," she said.

"Well, no," I interjected. "Legit would be if we were over twenty-one and they were our own IDs."

"You'll see; they're great!"

"So, how did you get a hold of them?" I quizzed.

"You know Dealer Dave?"

Of course I knew Dealer Dave. Well, I knew of him anyway. I'd only met him a couple times. He was the go to guy for weed, speed, and all your party needs. That was the word anyhow. We normally kept our distance from him and his crowd. Sure, L Squared was always up for a good party, but drugs were never invited. We weren't into that kind of thing.

"You got fake IDs from a drug dealer?" I asked, now

even more uneasy.

"They're not fake!" she insisted again.

"Oh my god! They're stolen!" I deducted.

"No. He has a ton of them. I think he pays people for them and then sells them for a markup."

"Yeah, right. Dealer Dave is a totally honest business man," I said.

"Whatev. Who cares how he got them? They're ours now, and they will definitely come in handy. Just wait 'til you see them. They're great. You're twenty-four."

"Twenty-four?" I laughed. "How old are you? Forty?"

"No. Mine says I'm twenty-two. It's perfect. We'll just vamp ourselves up a little. No one will ever know."

"Vamp up, huh?" I looked at her sideways. She looked so excited. Her cheer was always contagious, and catching it and going with it could rarely be avoided. She could always talk me into anything. "Okay," I gave in, giggling. "You're crazy, you know that?"

"Yep. That's why you love me!" She grinned.

"I guess it is." I laughed. "How did you pay for them?" I was worried her money was now blown on these IDs and the expensive tank top she just had to have from that store.

"Don't worry about it. They were cheap."

"How cheap?" I prodded.

"Like ten bucks a piece. It's no big deal," she said flippantly.

"Why were they so cheap?" I couldn't let it go. It sounded odd.

"He gave me a deal. Relax."

"A deal?" Oh great, a drug dealer had given her a deal. "Why would Dave give you a break on stolen goods?"

"Okay, again, they are not stolen," she insisted, "and I don't know. He likes me."

"Eew," I said, my mind immediately going to a bad place. "You didn't..."

"Eew!" she shouted. "No. Thanks so much for thinking

so highly of me. God! I just kind of told him we'd go out some time, but he probably got high after I left and forgot all about it. Who cares? Point is, we got 'em! Chill!"

"Yeah, okay. Sorry. I just figured you know, it's *you,* so..." I joked.

"Right! You suck," she said, tossing water at my face.

We laughed. We spent the next hour wading and splashing around.

Back in the room, the air conditioner had finally decided to cooperate. The cool air felt great. I closed my eyes and twirled around, plunking down on the cool bedspread. Just then, my anticipation got the better of me, and I couldn't wait to see the IDs Leah had gotten from Dealer Dave.

"Show me. Show me!" I cheered.

"Hold your horses," she said. Leah grabbed her duffle bag and started rummaging through.

"They're not in your wallet?" I asked.

"I didn't want my sister or my mom to find them," she said.

"Oh."

"Here they are!" She pulled a small makeup bag out of the duffle and unzipped it to reveal two driver's licenses. "Here you are!"

I grabbed the ID from her hand and studied it up and down, left to right. The photo really did look a lot like me, enough anyway to be believable. I read through all of Melissa's information. She was three inches taller than me, no big deal. That's what heels are for. Just as I was entertaining the possibilities of our new found ages, I noticed it. Blue eyes.

"Leah!" I said, disappointedly. "Her eyes are blue. How do I explain that?"

"Say you wear contacts now! Duh!" she responded. "My girl has green eyes and fluffy eyebrows, but I can totally pull it off." She flashed her ID toward me.

I giggled. The girl looked like she could be related to

Leah for sure, but they weren't really a match. With the right makeup, we could make it work.

"Yeah, I can see it," I agreed. "So you get to be Lindsey Martin from Texas? Lucky. They'll probably be less likely to question a Texas license."

"Yeah," she said, "but it'll be fine. You can be my awesome buddy, Melissa, from out of town."

"Yes, yes, I can, Lindsey Martin." I wondered if Lindsey and Melissa would mind if they knew we were using them to get liquor.

"I think I'll call you Missy, you know, when we're out."

"Sure thing, Linds!" I said. We laughed and went straight into our secret handshake, as we always did when we thought we had a brilliant plan all figured out.

We had four hours until the concert, which meant we only had three hours to get ready before we left. We wanted to get there early to get good parking and walk around the fair grounds. Brick Party Sundae was playing on the main stage at the Hadley County Fair. We'd heard about the fair from kids at school, and we'd been to the one in our own county, but Hadley was supposed to be really big and really fun.

"You know," I said after we finished up our handshake, "if we leave early enough, we could probably ride a ride or two before the show.

"Yes, we could," Leah said, rolling the thought around in her head. I saw a new thought coming to the forefront. "And," she went on, "if we get there even earlier, we could visit the beer garden and test out our new aliases."

"Beer garden?" I asked.

"Yep. Look." She had taken a fair brochure from the front when we checked in. She unfolded it to reveal a map of the fairgrounds. "See here? There is a beer garden right next to the main stage entrance. It's perfect."

"Cool," I said. I was thinking *what if we get busted and get kicked out before we even get to see BPS?,* but I didn't say it out loud. I decided to just go with it.

We took our showers and dried our hair, careful to take breaks every now and then from the blow-dryer so as not to heat the room up again. There's nothing worse than trying to put makeup on an already melting face. I let Leah do her face first, and then I asked her to do my eyes for me.

Upon last looks, we looked pretty great; a little on the skanky side, but definitely older, and definitely double take worthy. Leah was wearing her new tank with some distressed jeans, and I had on a blue top that laced up the center with a pair of tight, black dress pants. We posed together for a few self taken photos with my digital camera, packed our mini purses with our tickets, cash, new identities, lip gloss, and cell phones, and headed out the door.

The fair grounds were about four blocks from the motel, and we decided we'd walk there instead of driving, since we were hoping we'd be tipsy by the time the concert was over. Excitement and nerves were high. I was nervous anyway; Leah seemed oddly cool and calm about the scam we were going to be running.

As we walked, we got the expected reaction for two girls dressed like we were. A few horn honks and out the window hollers from some young guys, a bunch of dirty looks from passing females, and one stopped truck with three guys in it asking if we needed a ride. Of course Leah threw them a flirty smile and an exaggerated "depends on where you're going," to be cute, but I declined for the both of us. They were attractive, but no matter how attractive, I would never accept a ride from a stranger. That might sound very *first grade, stranger danger*, but I think it's a good rule to live by, especially if you want to keep living. I've seen the TV specials, and it is surprising how many serial killers are extremely good looking.

We got to the front gate and had to pay admission, even though we had concert tickets. A ten spot later, we were headed straight for the beer garden. It was hot and sticky;

cold beer sounded pretty great.

I looked around at all the lights and the rides. It wasn't dark yet, but the twinkling was still distracting. The screams and gleeful squeals of all the children made me smile. Then, I remembered why I'm not a huge fan of kids. A moose of a boy ran straight into me and smashed his cotton candy between himself and the right leg of my pants. I leapt back to assess the damage. There was a pink, sugary web stuck to my thigh. I brushed at it with my hand, but that just rubbed it into the fabric and made my hand sticky. The spot left behind glistened in the sunlight. It was there to stay until the next washing. All I could think was *I hope it gets dark soon so no one notices it.*

"Watch where you're going, lady!" the kid scolded. He recovered his cotton candy from his shirt and shoved a piece he plucked from it into his mouth.

"Oh, I'm so sorry," I said, mostly sarcastically.

"Jerk!" he yelled as he ran away into the crowd.

"Whoa, can you believe that kid?" I asked my best friend.

"What a little scum bag," Leah said. "You wanna try putting water on it?"

"No. That'll probably make it worse. It's pure sugar. It's cool. I'll live."

"Oh, hey! There it is," Leah said, pointing toward a canvas tent with an emblem of a famous beer brand on the side.

"Lead on!" I instructed.

We made our way to the tent entrance. There was a guy standing by the opening, checking IDs. We pulled ours from our purses. I gripped mine nervously in my hand. As Leah handed hers over for inspection, I realized I had forgotten my name; my fake name that is. I didn't remember who I was supposed to be. Adrenaline shot through my body. My arms felt limp, and my hands were clammy. I wanted to look at it. I wanted to study it again, but if I looked at it, I thought that might give me away. He would definitely know it wasn't mine if I was studying it before handing it over. He wrapped a bracelet around Leah's right wrist to signify that she was over twenty one, and he flagged her through.

Oh no! my head screamed. *He's gonna know! He's gonna know! Run!* But I didn't run. I stood there. He held his hand out for my driver's license. I gave it to him.

"Hi!" I said cheerily. Why did I have to speak? I shouldn't have said anything. It sounded forced. That one word could give me away. My "hi" made me sound guilty.

He didn't say anything back. He glanced at the picture on the ID and glanced at me. It was probably only two seconds, but it felt like an eternity. My insides were jelly. He handed the card back to me and sighed.

No! He sighed! He knows! Run! But I still didn't run.

He curled his fingers up, motioning for me to give my wrist to him. He slid the bracelet around and snapped it into place.

"Have fun," he said, and he waved me through the front.

He didn't know. We did it. We fooled the beer garden man. L Squared was on the way to beer town.

Leah ordered us two frothy beers from a girl dressed up like a beer wench. The outfit was pretty cute, but her blue hair didn't exactly go with the whole 1800s tavern motif inside the tent.

"You can get next," Leah said, handing me my plastic cup.

"Deal," I replied.

We clinked our cheap beer cups together and chugged it down. I walked over to the wench and ordered our second round. We chugged those and then sat down at a picnic table for a minute to let the effects kick in. I looked around and noticed that the place was pretty popular. There were couples and groups of friends huddled around the picnic tables that were placed all around the giant tented area. It was a great place to cool off. There were misters around the sides and giant fans placed strategically around the perimeter. My eyes went back to my friend, who was smiling at nothing for no reason in particular. She was just happy I guess.

"You think maybe we should have eaten something?" I asked Leah as I felt the cold sudsy beverage swish in my stomach.

"Nah!" She burped and laughed. "This is better. We'll get drunk faster and cheaper!" Her logic seemed perfectly sensible at the time.

I laughed with her and leaned to the side. It had been only a few minutes since the last beer, and I was already feeling a buzz.

"Ooh," I said, "I'm feeling all warm and buzzy."

"You mean warm and fuzzy?" Leah corrected.

"Yeah, that too." I laughed.

"Come on," she said. "We have half an hour before the show starts. Let's go get our seats and grab another drink.

"Good plan!"

We got up from the seating area and walked toward the tent exit. As we pushed through the flap, a burst of air came down on our heads from the fan above the opening. We were then assaulted once more by the incredible heat from the outside.

"Ugh!" Leah said painfully. "This heat is so gross."

"Thank God it'll be dark soon," I said. I then remembered my pants. I looked down at the cotton candy sugar splotch. It was barely noticeable. I grimaced, remembering for a second the kid who ran into me. I swayed to the side and almost lost my balance, which for some reason caused me to burst out laughing. Were I sober, almost falling over would probably have been more embarrassing than hilarious, but I wasn't sober, so the laughter continued.

"What are you doing?" Leah asked, having to grab my arm. "Come on, freak show." She laughed and linked her arm through mine.

We walked a few steps, feeling pretty good.

"Look!" Leah shouted. "Fun house! We have to go!"

"Yes!" I agreed loudly. "It's on!"

We waltzed up to the line and waited like a couple of giddy children. The two kids in front of us gave their tickets to the carnival attendant and went inside.

"Tickets!" Leah hissed. "We don't have tickets!"

"We need tickets?" I asked stupidly. Of course we needed tickets. It was a carnival attraction.

"Excuse me, sir, is there any way we could not pay with tickets?" Leah asked. I'm not sure why she asked; I'm assuming it was because she was already drunk. He scowled at her and pointed a skinny finger toward the ticket booth fifteen feet away. "Awesome!" Leah yelled. She grabbed my hand and skipped me over to the ticket booth. Normally two beers might not have done the trick, but we hadn't eaten since the treats at the coffee house, and we did throw the beer back awfully fast, so we were in a very happy place, which may have been annoying to those around us. Luckily, we didn't care.

"Hello, ticket booth person! And how are you this eve?" Leah greeted the lady in the ticket booth.

She gave Leah a dirty look and answered, "fine. How many?"

"Well, how many does it take for that?" Leah pointed to the fun house.

"This many," the lady said, holding up three fingers. She was talking to Leah like she was a child, but somehow Leah kept on, unphased.

"Great!" she said. "Then we'll take this many!" Leah held up three fingers on each hand and laughed.

"Six dollars, please," the lady said.

"That's a little steep, but we'll take it!" Leah squeaked. She turned to me for some cash. I gave her the six dollars. She handed the lady the five and the one I'd given her, and she got our tickets in return. "Thank you. Have a lovely night."

The lady scowled at us and chose not to respond.

"Man," Leah said, "I would hate to be the giant bug up her butt."

We laughed ridiculously loud and ran back to the fun house. Neither of us realized that we just spent six dollars just to look in some funny mirrors and walk through a swirling round about like a hamster. We didn't care.

"Here you are, sir." Leah handed over the tickets. The man put them into a box next to the entrance and waved us through.

We wove ourselves in and out of some punching bag sort of things hanging from the roof, made our way across two sliding beams, each moving in a different direction, went up some moving stairs, and found ourselves on the second story of the lamest fun house ever in a tiny room of misshapen mirrors. One made me look like I was ten feet tall with a giant head, the next made me look super squat and plump, and the last one had both effects giving me a giant head, giant hips, and skinny everything else. There were two others, but they weren't very well manufactured as neither of them looked out of the ordinary at all. We giggled like kids anyway. Apparently, beer made the fun house, well, fun. If we were sober, we would have demanded our money back. Actually, if we were sober, we wouldn't have paid to go inside, as anyone could clearly see that it wasn't worth it just from looking at it outside. We trotted gleefully to the pole at the end of the room that shot us down like firemen to the first floor. Then, we ran through the final obstacle, the turning wheel thingy. Definitely not worth six bucks, but at the time, it seemed like a great thing to do.

We laughed until our stomachs hurt. We sat outside the exit for a few moments to catch our breath and compose ourselves.

"What time is it?" I asked Leah.

"We only have ten minutes!" she yelled. "Let's go!"

"We're coming, Brick!" I squealed as we ran toward the

entrance for the main stage.

We got inside and looked for our seats. Because we bought the cheapest tickets we could find online, our seats were in the bleachers up in the back of the arena. We could see the stage really well though, and there were gigantic monitors on each side, so we would be able to see Brick's gorgeous face in close up when the cameras were on him. For now, there were giant ads on each one for the local sponsors.

"Beer. Let's get more beer," Leah suggested.

I got up and followed her to a beer cart. We already had the bracelets on from the beer garden, so the cart person didn't even ask for ID. It was easy. We got two each and went back to our seats in anticipation of the show. Leah quickly downed one of hers, but I sipped mine. I didn't want to waste all of my time going back and forth to the bathroom when my man, Brick Donovan, was on stage.

I could actually feel myself getting nervous. My heart raced as I thought about Brick and his band being right in front of me. Brick Party Sundae was actually there, in person, and they'd soon be so close to me. Yes, we were up in the nosebleeds, but still, I'd never been that close to a famous person before in my whole life, especially not someone as amazing and brilliant as Brick himself.

My head was swirling with excitement and daydreams.

"L!" Leah shouted. "I have to pee."

The opening band was tuning up. The vibrations from the few chords that were played tickled my ear drums and got my adrenaline pumping.

"You better go now!" I said. I didn't want either of us to miss any part of this great experience.

"Come with me," Leah pleaded.

"What? What about our beer?" I said.

"Chug it. Let's go."

"Agh!" I protested halfheartedly. I didn't want to down two beers that quickly, but I also knew I couldn't possibly hold three cups while I waited in line for Leah. I chugged one and held tight to the other. "I'll just hold mine and yours while you go, then we'll switch."

"Deal!" she said with urgency. She handed me her other cup. "Let's roll!"

We speed-walked around, searching desperately for the bathrooms. Finally we saw the large sign for the women's restroom. Leah ran inside only to find a line of six other women waiting.

"Dude!" Leah complained to me. "I really have to go!"

"It's fine. I'm sure they'll be fast," I comforted, but I was wrong. All of a sudden the beer hit my bladder too, and I was desperate and uncomfortable. The ladies took what seemed like forever to weed out. Finally, Leah made it to the front of the line.

"Okay, hurry," I said.

She went in, then I had no choice but to let the two girls behind me go ahead, since I had the stupid cups in my hands. I was potty dancing by the time Leah arrived to relieve me of beer guard duty. I handed her the beers and my silly mini purse and ran for the open stall. Victory was mine! I instantly felt a million times better. Unfortunately, that wouldn't be the last urgent pee run of the night. Turns out, beer on an empty stomach is not the best idea.

We got out of the bathroom just in time. Luckily for us, the opening band was a few minutes late taking the stage. We weren't actually sure who the first band was going to be. The tickets said *Brick Party Sundae and Special Guest.* Unless Special Guest was the name of a new band we'd never heard of, the identity of the opening band was a mystery.

As they took the stage, we instantly knew who they were. We'd seen them on TV before. The lead singer's purple hair gave them away. Her name was Melanie Rave. I'm sure that wasn't her birth name, but she was super cool, and she was the fantastic lead singer of the band Mel Says Go.

"It's Mel!" Leah shouted. "This is awesome!" She squeezed my hand and cheered.

We were both so excited. We danced around and sang along to the whole set. Melanie was incredible. Mel Says Go played about forty minutes and did almost their entire *Studio MelFunction* album. I had the CD in my car, and I had uploaded it to my mp3 player just days before. I loved Melanie. I envied her cool style and "don't give a crap" attitude.

The crowd went nuts for them. It seemed like all the concert goers and BPS fans were stoked by the Mel Says Go appearance. We even collectively were able to cheer Mel Says Go into an encore. It was amazing.

As soon as they left the stage after their encore song, I made a mad dash for the bathroom. Unfortunately, the line was even longer this time. It was a good thing I was drunk, or else I may have passed out from discomfort. On the other hand, if I hadn't been drinking, I wouldn't have had to go so badly. When I finally reached my stall, I heard a voice over the system asking if we were ready for some Brick Party Sundae. My heart sank. I was praying that my stupid bladder hadn't just made me miss Brick's entrance. I hurried along as fast as I could. Of course, I had to wash my hands. I never left a bathroom without washing my hands. I did a three second lather and rinse and ran for my seat. Leah was standing up in anticipation.

"You didn't miss it!" she shouted over the crowd. "They're coming on now!"

"I'm so excited!" I yelled.

We squealed ecstatically. The lights on the stage started flashing and going haywire. Then the crowd roared and cheered as the band settled into their places on stage. Once they got to their marks, the entire stage went black. Cameras flashed toward the darkness. I wasn't really conscious of it, but I had been holding my breath the entire time. The lights burst on, and there he was. Brick Donovan. He was beautiful. I took in a deep breath as I glared at this marvelous creature behind the microphone. He was wearing tight leather pants and a sheer black shirt, which was only buttoned up to his middle. His skin glistened in the bright lights.

"How are you doing tonight, Hadley?" He spoke into the microphone.

The crowd cheered and whistled. I stood, silent, taking it all in.

"I want to start off by saying how excited we are to be here with all of you," he went on. "This first song is dedicated to all you beautiful people here tonight."

I felt like he was talking right to me. We were far from him, but somehow, I thought he could see me, and he was speaking just for me. Completely crazy, yes, but it was how it felt.

The band started up, and the crowd went nuts. We all knew the song. It was their latest radio hit. People started jumping up and down and waving their arms up in the air. Leah grabbed my hand. We looked at each other and screamed a happy scream. We were actually there. We were witnessing, first hand, the brilliance that was Brick Party Sundae.

Brick sang so beautifully. His voice never faltered. He sounded almost as perfect as he did on his albums. Each song was welcomed by the crowd with intense cheers. The audience sang along to every tune, and we joined them.

An hour and two encores later, which seemed to pass in a millisecond, BPS was finished playing. My heart was swollen with joy. My best friend and I had just seen Brick Party Sundae live. It was the single most exciting thing we'd ever done.

As the crowd shuffled toward the exits, we sat for a moment and let the new calm fall over us. My ears felt numb and still rang from the decibel of the music we'd heard. My head felt sort of stuffy from all the sound, but it was a good feeling, an accomplished and satisfied feeling.

"That was incredible," I declared to my friend sitting next to me.

"To say the least," Leah said.

"Now what?" I asked her. I didn't really want the night to end. I was still high from all the excitement.

"Well..." her word lingered. She thought for a moment. "We could hit up that liquor store we saw walking over here and have ourselves a little after party."

"Excellent! You always have the best ideas!" I announced. I was still buzzing from the beer.

"I know!" She jumped to her feet and motioned for me to lead the way.

We walked, arm in arm, through the sea of people. We giggled and reminisced over the concert. it's not as if we would have already forgotten any piece of it, but we still had to have the "my favorite part was when" and "did you see when the" conversation. We smiled and talked about BPS dreamily all the way. It was like we floated out of the fairgrounds.

The air was warm but finally bearable. Street lights and car beams lit the small town. We made it to the liquor store just in time. They were closing in ten minutes. We picked out a cheap bottle of whiskey, and I handed Leah some cash and stood back to let her handle the purchase. Though our IDs worked fine at the fair, I wasn't so sure I could pull it off in front of a seasoned liquor clerk. She made some silly chit chat about the weather, complimented his shirt, and we were out the door with a seven dollar bottle of whiskey.

Back at the motel, we hit up the vending machines for mixers. We thought the machines would somehow be cheaper than buying a two liter soda at the liquor store, but as usual, we were wrong. It ended up costing us three dollars for two sodas, when we could have purchased a two liter for a dollar and change at the store. Oh well. We were still back on our way to drunk town.

We burst into our room, laughing and being chatty as ever. I plopped myself down on the bed and waited for Leah to mix our cocktails. I heard her unwrapping the plastic cups that rested in the bathroom next to the sink.

"Crap! Ice!" she yelled. "Never fear, Leah is here! I'll get it." She jogged over to the TV stand, put down the freshly opened cups, grabbed the ice bucket, and leapt out the door.

I giggled to myself and laid back onto the bedspread. I closed my eyes and then realized that I was laying on top of the nasty overused and likely under washed comforter of a flea bag motel.

"Eew!" I screamed and hopped up from the bed. I peeled back the comforter and checked over the sheets. They appeared clean. Satisfied, I sat back down. Leah quickly appeared back in the room with a full ice bucket.

"Ice is here!" She grinned wide and distributed some of the cubes into our plastic motel cups. The seal made a crackling sound as she opened the whiskey bottle. She poured generously and then added a splash of her soda to each. "Here's to the best night ever," she said, handing me a cup.

"And," I said clinking my cup to hers, "here's to out doing ourselves every day and making each night of our trip the best night ever."

"Here, here!" she said, raising her glass.

We both put our drinks to our lips and guzzled.

"Bah!" I gasped as the cheap alcohol stung my throat and burned its way down into my stomach. I could feel it attacking my insides. "That is harsh!"

"I know!" Leah agreed. She was wincing almost as hard as I was.

"So," I said, still reeling from the after taste, "want another?"

We both laughed and grimaced at the thought.

"No, but yes," Leah replied.

"Maybe mix them with more soda?"

"You think?" Leah said sarcastically.

She took our cups, walked back to the TV stand, which now served as our mixing station, and she poured a shot into each cup with a much more generous serving of cola.

"Okay. Let's try this again," she joked. She gave my cup back over and laughed at the sour expression that had commandeered my face.

I took the cup. This time, there were no cute toasts or clinking of plastic cups. We each took a deep breath and just chugged it down. It went a little more smoothly that way.

"See," Leah said victoriously, "that wasn't so bad."

"Wasn't so good either," I said back. It still had a nasty after taste, but that wasn't going to stop me from trying it again. I handed her my cup for round three, and we were off.

A couple cups later, we were pretty loopy. The rest of the night was spent laughing about nothing, talking about anything and everything, and watching bad, basic cable programming. The neighbor knocked on the wall once or twice because we were too loud, which managed to keep us quiet for about two or three minutes at a time. We tried, but the whiskey was talking for us, and its voice was very loud.

We passed out some time around three in the morning, which I'm sure our room neighbor was thankful for.

CHAPTER FIVE

Next thing I knew, I was rolling over with a pain in my head I hadn't felt in a very long time. I looked at the clock through murky vision. It read *8:04*.

"Water," I said to myself. I got up very slowly and dragged myself to the bathroom. I put my mouth to the faucet and turned the handle on the right side of the sink for cold water. It felt amazing on my tongue, but that feeling would be far too temporary. Satisfied, I rose from the sink only to be reminded that my head felt like it was about to explode. I thought I could actually feel my brain trying to free itself from my skull. My face felt numb and dry, and my entire body felt heavy and gross. I made my way back to my bed and slowly lowered myself back into it. I closed my eyes and prayed for sleep, but it didn't come. Oh the pain. Leah was snoring. I envied her.

An hour later, Leah woke up and headed for the bathroom in a similar fashion to the way I had. I heard the water running, and I pictured her guzzling from the tap as I had done. I placed my hand to my forehead in an attempt to stop the pain, but of course, my hand didn't have magic healing powers, so it didn't help in the least.

"Here," Leah said, walking over to me with a cup of water in one hand and a pill in the other.

"Oh, you read my thumping mind," I said as I held out my hand for the aspirin she was giving me.

"Yeah. I am so mad at us right now," Leah reported.

"Tell me," I agreed. I thought back to how we ended up in this dismal state. The idea of alcohol made me want to visit the bathroom again. My stomach was empty though, and I had nothing to offer. I immediately regretted all the drinking on an empty stomach. It was rare that I had this kind of hangover. I was way beyond the "eat and you'll be fine" rule I'd come up with. Then I also recalled the grand rule of drinking, "beer before liquor, never been sicker", and I felt defeated.

"Maybe if we eat, or sleep, or man... I have no idea how to fix this," Leah said.

I tried to smile, but it wouldn't come. All I could think about was how badly I wanted to remove my brain and put it on ice, or dunk my head in a bucket of freezing cold water. Then, a plan broke through the surface.

"We have to get in the pool. Like now," I said.

"No, no, no," Leah protested. "I can't move. Are you kidding?"

"No, it will be good. Trust. Let's do it," I insisted.

Leah exhaled loudly and forced herself over to her bathing suit.

"Fine," she huffed.

Ten minutes later, we were shuffling our feet across the poolside concrete, being hit from every direction by the cruel beams of the sun.

"Alright," I said as I removed my shorts and flip flops, "we have to just jump in."

"No," Leah argued.

"Yes. It is the only way," I told my hesitant buddy.

She frowned in my direction, shook her head, and let out a deep breath, which meant she was on board but not happy about it.

We scooted to the very edge of the deep end. We looked at each other, gave a head nod, held our breath, and made the leap. I felt the cold rush over me. It was terrible and fantastic at the same time. My head emerged from the water and I wiped my eyes, looking for Leah.

"Ah!" She screamed as she popped to the surface. "That is cold!"

I laughed. Then I realized I was able to laugh now. I dunked my head under. I let the cold water soak into my hair. It felt like an icepack for my angry brain. My headache was instantly better, not gone, but definitely better. The water revived me and gave me a sense that I could go on with the day and maybe not die. Hangovers are evil, plain and simple. Why does there have to be such a severe punishment for having a little harmless fun?

My head felt better, but I still had a nauseas stomach that needed attention.

"Food and coffee?" I ran the idea past Leah.

"Yes!" she agreed.

"Quick shower and then cafe run," I added.

We hopped out of the pool and walked back to our room. Half hour later, we were dressed and ready to go. We decided to forego hair drying and makeup and head straight for the caffeine and breakfast treats.

The cafe we'd been to the day before was, luckily for us, not very busy. I gave a quick glance at the menu, and I was delighted to see they offered our oh so favorite day after drinking treat, breakfast burritos. They were six bucks a piece, which would make our orders over nine a piece, and then there was the tip jar, but I didn't care how much they were. I needed it; I wanted it; I was getting it. We ordered iced lattes and our burritos, and I had the girl charge the order to my bank card. I then placed a couple dollars I had loose in the tip jar. We waited by the "order pickup" sign for our goodies. I was relieved that my head wasn't pounding, but it still felt like it was spinning slowly in one direction and like I was going another. I needed that breakfast burrito... bad.

Just as I was dreaming of how that burrito was about to

change my life, my attention got drawn toward the door. A familiar person walked up to the counter to place his order. It was the gorgeous boy, Blue, who we'd met in this very spot the day before.

"Oh my god," I whispered, putting my head down.

"What?" Leah asked, and then, noticing Blue said, "oh..."

"We have to get out of here. Where's our food?" I asked impatiently. There was no way I was going to let that gorgeous guy see me with frizzy, half dry hair and zero makeup.

"Calm down. It's no big. Talk to him," Leah said.

"Seriously? Look at me."

"You look fine. He's gonna come over here when he's done ordering. You're gonna have to say something," she said.

"No I don't."

"Come on. Don't be a cowardly tiger. Just say hi or something," Leah insisted.

"Lion," I corrected.

"What?"

"You mean lion, not tiger," I explained.

"Whatever." Then, she went on quietly, "here he comes."

I put my head down further. I don't think my neck had ever bent that much before.

"Oh hey," Blue greeted. "L, right?"

NO!!!! My dizzy head screamed. I had to look up now. There was no other option.

"Oh, right!" I said cheerily, looking up at his perfect face. "How are you?"

"Great," he said, "just getting the usual for the crew."

"Oh, cool, cool," I replied.

"So, you girls have fun at the concert last night?" he asked.

Wow, he remembered what we were doing last night.

Maybe he is interested, I thought.

"Yeah," I said, "almost too much fun." I was attempting to make a funny, and hopefully cute, excuse for our lousy appearances.

"Nice," he said. "So you heading home today then?"

"No," Leah chimed in, "we're heading over to Stover for the show tonight."

"No way!" Blue said loudly. His voice boomed through my head, but I didn't let on that I was pained by it. "I'll be out in Stover tonight too," he continued.

"Really?" Leah went on, "well, maybe we should meet up or something." She winked at me and tried to slyly elbow me, but I'm pretty sure it wasn't as subtle as she meant it to be.

"Yeah, sure. Let me give you my number. Hit me up after the show," he directed toward me.

Yes!

"Yeah," I said giddily, reaching for my cell. "Okay, go ahead."

He recited his ten digit phone number, and I typed his name as *Blue :)*. It was saved, and I had every intention of using it.

"Cool," he said. "So, I'll talk to you tonight then?"

"Yeah, definitely," I replied, grinning like a geek.

"Leah and L," the barista said, placing our order up on the counter.

"That's us!" Leah claimed.

"Well," I said, "we have to go get ready, and check ourselves out of our room, and get on the road."

"Alright." Blue smiled a sweet smile. "You girls have a safe drive, and I guess, well... tonight."

"Yep. Tonight," I repeated.

"See ya," he said, waving.

"Bye," Leah and I said, almost in unison again.

We carried our stuff out to my car. We waited until we got in before squealing like little girls.

97

"Not bad for a cowardly tiger," Leah said.

"Lion," I reminded her.

"Right. Lion. Whatever." She laughed.

Back in our room, we chowed down our breakfast burritos, sipped our coffee, and took our sweet time getting ready. We weren't in much of a hurry. Checkout wasn't until one, and the drive to Stover was just under two hours, so we had plenty of time. Good thing we had time, because I don't think, in our sluggish state, we could have gone much faster.

I took a few minutes to call my mom too. I told her all about our great night, skipping the parts about the fake IDs and all the whiskey. She wouldn't have been too hard on me, but she would have felt obligated to tell me how dangerous it was to run around with fake driver's licenses and get smashed in public. I would have heard all about the dangers of our unfamiliar surroundings and the possibility of being stopped by someone who carded us, or worse, the police. After lecturing for ten minutes or so she would say something like "I trust you to make good choices. Just be careful," and that would be that. I just didn't have it in me at the time to go through the motions, so I chose to omit the illegal parts. I figured I'd tell her later, like when we got home, and avoid the talk all together. As long as we were safe, she was happy.

By the time we had to leave the place, we were both feeling much better. We grabbed a couple overpriced waters from the vending machine, and we were back on the road.

The sun seemed exceptionally bright that day. It reflected off everything we came across. I was taking full advantage of my sunglasses and my car visor. Unfortunately, my trusty sidekick fell asleep ten minutes into our trek, and I was forced to wind my way down the highway alone. I put some music on low and kept my eyes on the hot asphalt stretched out in front of me.

I couldn't help but let my mind wander toward thoughts of Blue. I wondered what it might be like when we got together. I wondered where we would go and what we would do. I imagined he had an equally good looking friend for Leah, and the four of us would hit it off perfectly and laugh our way into the night. The night would turn into the next day and the next day would turn into the next year, and, eventually, the four of us would be house shopping together in a cute, beachside community in California. Then I remembered Amanda and her new boyfriend, Travis, were beachside somewhere in sunny Cali, and I wondered if we'd run into them someday. Amanda would somehow seem less annoying in the ocean air, and she and Leah would get along great because they'd both have great guys. We'd have ocean view barbecues and play volleyball, three on three, in the warm sand. I caught myself smiling as I daydreamed, but I didn't drop the smile; I just kept on planning our beautiful perfect lives together.

Reality then set in. What if he didn't like me? What if he was just trying to be nice, or worse, what if he was interested in Leah? I tried to shake the negative out of my head and focus on the fun ahead. Leah and I were going to see Brick Party Sundae. Again! I still couldn't believe how great the show was the night before. I could only imagine how amazing it would be the second time. I wondered what Brick would be wearing this time. Then I imagined what it might be like if somehow we got closer this time, and Brick picked me out of the crowd. He'd pull me up on stage and profess his undying love to me in front of a roaring audience. I could hear the hearts of four hundred girls breaking as Brick pulled me to him.

"Dude," Leah's voice cut in over my ridiculous fantasy. "Where are we?"

"We're almost there, I think. Here, look at the map. Tell me which exit again." I handed her the computer printout of the day's route.

"Okay. We are at McMillan, and we need Lerner to get to town center, which should be..." she said scanning the map, "somewhere in the next few exits."

Just as she folded the map back in half, a sign appeared. *Lerner Ave. 4 mi.*

"Ah ha!" she shouted, pleased with herself. "There it is!"

"I see," I said, chuckling at my friend's statement of the obvious.

We arrived in Stover a little after three. We hadn't booked a room for the night, so then came the interesting part. We had to search for a decently priced place to stay. We drove around in circles, looking at all the hotel, motel, and inn signs we came across, trying to determine where to stop. Some of the signs had prices posted on them. Most seemed sort of reasonable, under the sixty dollar mark, but none of them looked all that appealing, and surprisingly, a lot of them didn't have any vacancies. After driving around for twenty minutes or so, we came across the Starlight Inn, which looked less dilapidated than the other cheap choices, had a vacancy light on, and a rate of forty nine dollars per night posted on the board outside.

"Can we do forty nine?" I asked Leah.

"Yeah. I guess. I mean, that's the best rate we've seen. We could always go back to that Shady Lane Motel place we saw and ask them for their rates at the counter before we decide," Leah said.

"Uh, no. It has the word *shady* right in the title. I don't think we're staying there," I joked.

"Okay then. Let's do this," Leah decided.

We parked near the front of the inn and walked inside to the front desk clerk, who happened to be an early twenty-something guy with a great smile and super cute dimples. I looked to Leah to see if she had noticed Mr. Cute Smile, and she was blushing. She obviously hadn't missed it. I made note of his gold colored name tag. Marcus.

"Hi," I greeted him. "You have rooms available, right?"

"We only have a few left. You picked a good time to come in," he said.

"Well, then we would like to take one of those rooms off

your hands," I advised.

"I can do that for you." He started typing away at his keyboard. "It looks like we only have singles left at forty nine per night plus tax. You only need one night?

"Yeah," I answered.

"Alright. Is one queen okay?"

"Sure." I looked to Leah as I said it, and she nodded in compliance. "We'll take it."

"Great. I just need your ID and a credit card, and I need you to fill out this form." He handed me a form to fill in my name and car description.

My brows furrowed as I tried to remember my license plate number. It came to me, and I completed the paper. I reached into my purse and grabbed my driver's license and credit card for the cute boy to glance over.

"Uh," he said, holding my license in one hand and the card in the other, "the names don't match. Is this you?" He turned the license back toward me.

It wasn't me! It was Melissa Scholl from Mississippi! I had given him my new fake ID by mistake.

"Oh, wow. No. Sorry. Uh, that's my, uh sister's. Here's mine. Hold on. Sorry. Oh, God." I fumbled desperately through my wallet and found the right one. I could feel the heat coming off my face. I knew I had turned bright red. I finally found my own driver's license and handed it over the desk. He gave back the fake and loosely studied the real one.

"Laverne... that's an interesting name."

"Yeah." As if it were even possible, my face got even redder. "People just call me L."

"Oh," he said, grinning. "Cool. So, your sister's ID, huh?" He laughed. "It's cool. I had one too before I turned twenty-one in April. I always used my older brother's. Is that Melissa person really your sister?"

"No. Not really." I giggled nervously, still completely embarrassed. Leah laughed at my stupidity as well. Thank goodness this Marcus guy was young and cool. A stern grown-up type may have taken the fake away from me, or turned me in for fraud. Who knows.

I turned to Leah to say something, as I was clearly now out of words.

"Well," she said, "that was fun. Anyway, need anything else from us?" Not really the words I would have used, but at least she said something.

"No. Hang on one sec. I'll activate your keys. Two keys?"

"Sure," she replied.

"Alright then," he said, smiling. He swiped two key cards through a funny little machine. "You are in room 207. You'll want to park somewhere out in the front lot, bring your bags through here, and take that elevator to the second floor." He pointed to the elevators down the hallway. "You'll take a right out the elevator and it will be just a few down on the left side."

His instructions were probably very helpful, but I wasn't letting them sink in. My head was still reeling from the ID flub. I felt so stupid. I'm positive he didn't care, and it was no big deal, but certain things got me turned upside down pretty easily. I just stared at the floor.

"Okay," he continued, "you're all set. Here is your credit card back and your key cards. If you need anything else, feel free to hit the front desk button on your room phone. I'll be here 'til six."

Leah elbowed me to snap me out of it. I was still staring at the floor, and the poor guy was trying to hand me my stuff.

"Oh," I laughed like a moron. "Thanks." I took the cards from his hand and placed my stupid driver's license back in my bag.

"Uh, wait," Leah said, stopping me from moving on. She turned to the hotel clerk. "You wouldn't happen to know where we can get BPS tickets for tonight, would you?"

Tickets! We didn't have tickets yet for the show that night. The show started in a mere five hours, and we didn't have tickets!

"Well, I'm pretty sure you can get them at the arena. The box office should be open," he said.

"Okay, yeah. Where might one get tickets if they were looking to get them, say, cheaper?" Leah asked. Me, I was embarrassed over an ID mix up, Leah, on the other hand, had no shame.

"Uh... I guess there will be scalpers outside before the show," he whispered, though no one else was around.

"Excellent!" Leah said.

"You know," Marcus went on, "I happen to be a pretty big BPS fan myself, and I have been trying to find someone to go with me. Maybe I can tag along with you two?"

"Sure!" Leah didn't waste any time. She obviously thought this guy was worth getting to know, and so I went along with it for her sake.

"Yeah, come with," I said, putting the previously awkward incident behind me.

"Awesome! Well, I'm off at six, so maybe I can swing by your room after I change, and we can pre-party or whatever."

"Okay!" Leah said with no hesitation. My thought was of course, *stranger danger*, but Leah apparently hadn't thought twice about inviting a strange guy over to our hotel room.

"Neat," I said, wearily.

"Cool. See ya then," Marcus said.

We went to the car to do a better parking job and collect our stuff. As we got in, I just had to poke Leah and ask her what she was thinking.

"Seriously? You're gonna invite some random dude up to our room, like where the bed is?" I asked.

"Uh, yeah. So?" She looked at me blankly. "What's the big deal? One, he works for the hotel, so it's not like he's gonna do anything shady at his place of business, and two, he's like really cute and doesn't exactly look like a psycho killer to me."

"Really? What does a psycho killer look like?"

"I don't know!" Leah answered, annoyed. "Not like that."

"You're nuts! Whatever. If this guy wants to murder someone, I'll just step out and leave you guys to it. It was a pleasure being your friend," I joked. I was half giving into her crazy plan. It wasn't as if I ever had much choice once Leah decided to do something.

"Oh thanks. He's not gonna kill anyone. Besides, don't you think it might be a good idea to have a man around when we go try to buy tickets from shady, street dudes tonight?"

"Fine. But seriously, if he's a psycho, you're on your own, buddy." I laughed. "I mean, really, if I open the door, and he has a chainsaw..."

"Okay!" she yelled. "I get it. And speaking of cute strangers, when are you going to call Blue?" She elbowed me playfully.

I couldn't help but smile at the mention of his name. "I don't know," I said, still smiling like an idiot. "Later, I guess. Whatever. Shut up. I need to concentrate on re-parking my vehicle." I was trying to deflect, but it clearly didn't work.

Leah laughed at my childlike giddiness. I found my car a new spot close to the hotel's main doors. We got our things from the trunk and hauled them through the lobby. I nodded politely at Marcus, who was waving at us from behind the counter as we walked through. I shook my head and sighed.

The elevator was slow. It seemed to take an unreasonably long time to go just one floor up. It thudded as we arrived at the second floor. We jumped out and went to the right like Marcus said, and we found our home for the night.

We were pleasantly surprised by the room. It was a lot nicer than the one we'd stayed in the night before. There weren't any undesirable smells, and the air conditioner was already working just fine. The carpets looked fairly new, and the place was sparkly clean. The TV set was a fossil, and the drapes could have used a little care, but other than that, we were pretty well set. We'd definitely found more for our dollar this time. I was really hoping that the rest of our trip would prove so lucky.

"Maybe we should sit down and crunch some numbers," I suggested to Leah. We hadn't really been paying attention to our spending as much as we needed to. I was a little worried that we weren't going to be able to stick to our trip allowance.

"Crunch some numbers?" Leah asked. "Who are you, my accountant?"

"Oh, ha ha, okay, but we seriously should sit down and figure out what we have compared to our projected cost over the next eight days."

"Projected cost? Wow. You really do sound like an accountant." She laughed and winked at me, but she got more serious when I didn't laugh with her. "Okay, yes. You're right. Let's do that, but not right now. Right now, let's discuss what our plan is for tonight, how we're getting there, and how cute Marcus is."

"Marcus is cute. I guess the plan is we go, what, like an hour early maybe and find us a scalper dude. And what do you mean how are we getting there? I have my car, nerd."

"Right, but you aren't gonna want to drive after a few cocktails..." Leah said, stretching her last word to make it sound more enticing. She reached in her duffle bag and pulled out the remainder of our whiskey from the night before.

"No! No way. That stuff is toxic! I'm still hung over. Are you nuts?" I felt like I was asking her that a lot the last couple days.

"Yes, yes I am." She smiled an evil smile and got two cups from the dresser top.

"That is a terrible idea. Let's wait a little while before we drink again."

"Like an hour?" She was hopeful.

"No, like a week," I responded, laughing.

"An hour it is," she decided. She snuggled the bottle up to the glasses and let it rest there.

"Let's go get food," I suggested. "I'm starving. Something cheap though."

"Okay," she agreed.

We left the hotel and hit up a nearby drive thru. Six dollars each later, we were full and happy, and we had sodas to use for mixers. I, of course, had once again been talked over to the dark side by my good friend, Leah.

A few drinks, some hair teasing, a paint job, and an outfit change later, we were ready to go. The bottle was empty, and we were well on our way back to drunk town. Half past six, there was a knock at the door.

"Oh my god!" Leah squealed. "That's him."

"So," I said, rolling my eyes, "answer it. Check for a chainsaw before you let him in!"

"Shh!" She shushed me, checked herself over in the mirror once more, and skipped over to the door. She peered through the peep hole. "No chainsaw," she whispered back to me.

"Well then, by all means." I motioned for her to go ahead.

"Hi," she said flirtatiously as she swung the door open.

"Good evening," Marcus greeted her. He handed her a bottle of something I couldn't see just yet and came in.

As they came closer, I noticed that Leah was hauling a brand new bottle of whiskey. It was a better label than the cheap stuff we'd been guzzling. I might have wondered why a twenty-one year old was bringing eighteen year olds booze, but I was already half looped, and I wasn't really in code deciphering mode. The usual, semi cynical and always leery me might have thought he was trying to get my friend drunk and take advantage. Then again, obviously he knew we liked to drink. I did give him my mock ID earlier.

I jumped up and inspected the bottle. I took it from Leah and cracked it open myself so I could make sure it was in fact brand new and never opened. It was sealed. I guess the *stranger danger* part of me was still vaguely present.

"Thank you for bringing this, Marcus. That was super nice of you," I said.

I looked around the room and realized we didn't have any more soda. I volunteered to go to the vending machine. Marcus informed me that I would have to go downstairs to the lobby machine as the one on our floor was broken. I grabbed a few bucks from my purse and took off for the lobby.

I hopped in the elevator and hit the button for the main floor. The doors slid shut slowly, very slowly. I then remembered just how slow the stupid elevator was.

"Wait, wait!" I yelled at the doors. I hit the button to open them, but it didn't cooperate. I was stuck in there for the slow journey down. I groaned, frustrated. I then laughed to myself when I looked back at the buttons and realized I was pushing the door close button. I leaned myself against the back wall and settled in for the ride. What seemed like ten minutes later, I was in the lobby.

I followed the sign to the vending machines and selected a generic cola. I did it twice, costing me two dollars, and satisfied I had plenty for us to share in mixed drinks, I took off for the elevator. Back in the elevator, I realized once again that I didn't want to be there. This time I hit the correct button to open the doors, and I got myself out. I headed for the stairs and whisked myself and my loot up to the second floor.

I had to knock on the door, because I didn't bring my key card. It took Leah a suspiciously long time to open the door for me, but when I got inside the room, everything seemed to be in place, including their clothing, so I didn't ask why it took so long to answer.

I handed the sodas over to Leah, and she mixed us up

some drinks. A couple later, we were calling a cab to take us to the Stover Heights Arena. Marcus said it wasn't very far from the hotel, so it wouldn't cost us much in fare. It ended up costing me twelve dollars, which to be honest, kind of irked me, but I didn't say anything. Leah of course said she'd pay for the ride back, so I just let it roll off. I think I was more annoyed that he didn't offer to chip in.

Walking up to the side entrance, I felt nervous. I was worried that we wouldn't find someone with tickets, and at the same time, I was worried that we would. The booths at the side entrance were closed, and it was dimly lit on that side. Marcus insisted that if there were going to be scalpers, that's where they'd be. We waited there for about ten minutes, and then, sure enough, a guy walked up to us and asked quietly if we were buying. It felt super seedy.

"You looking to buy?" he asked. It sounded like he was slinging smack.

"Yeah, man," Marcus said. "How much?"

"Forty per," the guy said, looking over his shoulder.

"Forty!" I accidentally yelled. I continued more quietly, aware that I may have drawn attention. "Forty? That's insane. They're twenty online."

"Look, do you want 'em or not?" the guy asked.

"Not," I said.

"L!" Leah said, trying to shush me.

"No, Leah. Forty is ridiculous. I won't pay it."

"L, be cool," Marcus said.

Had he really just told me to be cool? That pissed me off.

"How about thirty, man. Can you go thirty?" Marcus asked the guy.

"These are good seats. They're worth the forty. The shows sold out. You can't get seats like these. Guaranteed." The seedy guy darted his eyes around again, checking the surroundings.

"How good? Can I see them?" Marcus put his hand out.

The guy handed him one ticket. "You know, I'm taking a chance splitting these up as it is," the guy said. "I have four tickets, and you only want three. I mean, you know how hard it's gonna be to unload just the one?"

"These aren't that great, man," Marcus reported. "They're nosebleed. I shouldn't even give you the twenty you paid for 'em." Marcus handed the ticket back to the guy.

"Okay, okay," the guy gave in. "Thirty. Whatever. Give me ninety bucks, you got yourselves some tickets."

"Girls?" Marcus looked to us for our cash as he took some cash out of his wallet.

"Fine," I said, feeling totally swindled. Leah had sworn scalpers were cheaper. I should have listened to my gut and just gotten the tickets off the internet. Now I was worried. This show was sold out. It was posted all over the ticketing windows. What if the next shows were sold out too? I wasn't about to overpay for every ticket I bought. I pulled the money from my purse and angrily slammed it down into Marcus' hand.

"Jeez, L, take a chill," he said.

Be cool; take a chill; this guy was really working hard to win me over. I wasn't feeling him, at all. I was actually kind of annoyed with Leah, being that she was the one who invited him.

He handed our cash to the creepy man and gathered our tickets. The guy nodded a thank you nod and took off toward the street in a hurry.

"Alright, girls," Marcus said, obviously pleased with himself. "Let's go on in."

He handed each of us a ticket. I inspected mine to see where we were sitting.

"Section 7, Row R, is that good?" I asked him as we walked.

"Row R?" Leah asked. "My ticket says Row Q!"

"What? No way!" I grabbed for her ticket.

"Yeah, mine too. I'm in Q," Marcus said.

"So what, I'm like behind you guys?" I asked, my anger rejuvenated.

"I guess so," Marcus said. "The seats are close, so you should be right behind us. No big." Just when I thought Marcus couldn't get more annoying, he had to say that.

"No big?" I asked. "Yeah, it's a big! Switch with me, Marcus. Leah and I want to sit together."

"L, it's really not that big of deal. You're right behind us," Leah said.

"What? Seriously?" I couldn't believe my best friend was ditching me on our girls only road trip for some stupid desk clerk with a bad attitude.

"L," she continued in a whisper, "come on. I'll make it up to you." She pointed her eyes toward Marcus. It was code for she really liked him and wanted me to take a backseat. Normally, the cue was accepted, as we usually weren't in a city we didn't know, surrounded by a bunch of strangers. She was now asking too much. It didn't seem fair.

"You owe me," I said, letting her off way to easily.

"Thank you!" she squeaked.

Leah grabbed my hand with her left hand and Marcus' with her right. We gave our tickets to the guy at the turn-style, got scanned by a wand, and flagged through. Once we got to our seats, it was as if I disappeared. Leah turned back one time to see how I was doing in my seat alone, and from then, it was as if I wasn't there at all. I guess Mr. Scalper wasn't able to unload that ticket after all, as no one ever showed up to sit in the seat to the immediate left of mine. I tried to make small chit chat with the people to the right of me, but they were clearly on a date, so I didn't bother them too much. I, of course, told them that I was there with my best friend but that there had been some seating mix up. I pointed to Leah and tried to get her attention to introduce her, but she was all enthralled with Dimples, so I gave up. The couple I was talking to probably didn't believe me. I was the weird Brick Donovan stalker fan who came to concerts alone.

I felt lonely and stupid.

When the first act came on, I was pleased to see that it was Mel Says Go again. Mel pretty much did a repeat of the night before. It was just as awesome as it was the first time, except this time, I had to experience it by myself. I danced and sang along and pretended to be totally stoked on it, but the entire night felt ruined, and I couldn't get over it. As I watched Marcus and Leah paw each other to a slow song, I wondered if maybe I was jealous. Normally, I would be excited for Leah if she met someone she liked. I would usually be just as giddy as she was about it, but this time, she'd actually pushed me aside for someone. In all the time I spent with Greg, I always made sure Leah was a priority and that she never felt like a third wheel. She was never left out. This was bad; I wasn't even a third wheel, I was non-existent. I decided that I wasn't jealous; I was just plain angry. This trip was for us. I didn't mind if she wanted to make new friends along the way, but I never expected her to ditch me like this, to literally leave me behind. My anger killed my buzz, which made me feel even worse. I was sober and completely irritated.

I managed to continue on with my good time facade. Before I knew it, Brick was onstage, looking even sexier than he had the previous night. I tried to push my bad feelings out of my mind and let myself be engulfed by the music. I closed my eyes and let his voice wash over me. It wasn't any kind of instant or magical cure, but it did soothe me slightly. And then, it was over. Brick was done, the couple next to me wanted to get past me so they could get home and do who knows what, and Leah and Marcus were already moving toward the stairs. Were they seriously about to leave me?

"Hey! Leah!" I yelled after her.

She turned around and laughed. "L! I turned around and didn't see you. Did you move?"

Seriously? She didn't see me? I was sitting right behind her. More like, she didn't remember me.

"Uh, no, I didn't." I walked grumpily down the stairs to where they were.

"What do you say we go back for a night cap?" Marcus suggested.

"I'm pretty tired. Maybe you guys can hang out tomorrow?" I countered, trying to be as polite as possible. I'm not sure why I bothered with politeness; they certainly weren't being considerate of me. Mean just wasn't my way.

"Or we could just go back to the hotel and see how we feel once we get there," Leah said as she squeezed my arm.

"Sure. We'll see, but I am seriously tired, so..." I said, letting a hint that there was no way I was going to agree with this linger in the air.

I walked behind the cozy new couple. We had to walk a ways away from the stadium to catch a cab. There were too many people lined up right outside the place. We finally found an empty taxi. I sat in silence all the way back as the two of them whispered and giggled to each other. As we arrived at the hotel, I went to open the door and escape the tight space, but I was stopped by Leah's hand.

"L, can you get this? I didn't bring enough cash," Leah said.

"I got the last one," I reminded her. "I thought you were getting next."

"Well, I'll get the *next* next. Sorry."

"What about Marcus?" I asked. He hadn't even offered to pay.

"Oh, yeah," he said, "I don't have enough. Sorry."

"Fine." I took the money out of my purse and gave it to the driver. He handed me back some change, from which I counted out a tip for him. I thanked him, and we all piled out.

I took the stairs, and the two love birds took the super slow elevator to spend some alone time together. When they got to the room, I was already in my pajamas and ready to call it a night. I couldn't wait to start over in a new day. This day cost me almost three times as much money as it was supposed to, and being that I had pretty much the worst time ever, I felt robbed.

"Hey, L, can Marcus stay for a drink?" Leah asked me.

"Leah, I'm pretty beat. Can you maybe just see him later?"

"Well, yeah, but see he did bring this whiskey, and we should at least have one more drink. Please," she begged.

"Fine," I gave in, this time letting some of my steam come out in my voice. "One drink. That's it. Then it's nighty night."

"Deal!" she agreed. She poured all of us a drink.

I downed mine in a hurry, hoping that it would prompt them to do the same and end this terror of a night. Unfortunately, they didn't notice. They just kept on laughing, and talking, and drinking, and annoying. There was only one bed and one desk chair, so there wasn't much sitting room. I was forced into the corner desk chair of course, and they sat side by side on the bedspread. I saw him whisper something to her, and she then sauntered over to me.

"L, do you think maybe you could give us a little alone time?" Leah asked.

"What?" I'd had enough. "Alone time? Are you joking? Where am I supposed to go? It's almost midnight; nothing's open. Plus, I'm exhausted and just wanna go to bed."

"Come on, L. Just for a little bit," she went on.

"No. You want me to leave the room that I paid for, yes, *I* paid for. It's on *my* credit card. You haven't given me your share yet. Come to think of it, you still haven't paid your share of last night either."

"L, I said I'd get you back. I'll get you back." She looked at me sideways.

"Yeah, okay, well, even so, I paid for this room, and I paid for that bed, and I'm gonna sleep in it. You want me to leave the room in the middle of the night, with nowhere to go, so you can get all kinds of who knows what in the bed that I'm supposed to sleep in tonight? No. Besides, doesn't

Romeo over there have like an employee discount or something. Have him get you two a room if you need to hook up so bad."

"L, you're being really uncool," she complained.

"I'm being uncool? Do you want to talk about my night? I didn't have an ounce of fun tonight. I've been playing backseat the whole time just so you could have your little date, and now you're calling me uncool because I don't think it's a good idea to give up my space so my best friend can have sex with a stranger? You don't know him! And you're treating me like crap, so you want to talk uncool, look in a mirror," I said angrily. I was pretty loud, but I'm sure even if I wasn't, Marcus would have heard me anyway. The room wasn't that big.

"Maybe I should go," Marcus said. Finally! The boy took a hint.

"No, wait," Leah said, trotting back to his side. "Can you get us a room?" she asked him. Unbelievable. Instead of staying to work this out, she was really going to go off and hook up with a complete stranger.

"Yeah," he said, "I'll go see about it." He got up and left the room.

"Seriously, L," Leah said, turning to me, "what is your problem?"

"Wow, Leah, if you can't see it, then maybe I don't know you as well as I thought I did."

"What is the big deal?" she asked. "I really like this guy."

"Leah, you don't even know him. He lives hours away from you, and you'll probably never see him again. You really think he's going to take you seriously if you sleep with him tonight? And obviously he doesn't have any respect for you or for himself because he wouldn't have asked you to kick your best friend out in the street if he did. He doesn't have enough money to pitch in for a cab, but he has enough to pay for a sex room? For someone he just met? He's sleazy.

You're better than that."

"God, L, why can't you just be happy for me?"

"Happy that you're going to have another one night stand? Oh yeah, I'm real proud." I probably shouldn't have said it that way, but that's how it came out.

"Is that what you think of me? I'm easy?"

"Well what would you call it?" I said with venom. Again, probably shouldn't have said that, but I was mad, and it's pretty much the truth. I didn't actually want to hurt her though; I just wanted her to get it.

"Whatever. I'll be back in the morning." She grabbed the half empty bottle of whiskey and went out the door.

I sat, fixed in the chair for what seemed like forever. I was feeling so many things. We hadn't ever fought like that before. I was feeling hurt and angry, and I was also feeling guilty. I wasn't responsible for how she'd treated me the whole night, and yes, I was angry about it, but I never meant to make her feel judged. I didn't want her to make a mistake and sleep with this guy. It was dangerous for her physically and emotionally to keep putting herself out there like that, but I would have never called her easy to her face. That was just mean, and I felt horrible about it.

The angry part of me outweighed the guilty part, and I went to bed mad. I was glad that I was sleeping in a sex free bed, but I was really worried about my friend spending the night with a stranger.

As I lay there, worrying about Leah, Blue popped into my head. In all the mess, I had forgotten to call Blue! I immediately jumped out of bed and leapt to my phone. It was almost one in the morning. It was definitely too late for a phone call. I went back and forth over it for a minute. I didn't want to call so late, but I really didn't want him to think I forgot about him. I finally determined a text would be appropriate.

So sorry. Things got a little crazy. Hope you had a good night. -L

I waited a moment, but there was no response. Feeling even worse than before, I dragged myself across the hotel carpet, placed the phone on the nightstand, and got back in bed. Then came a chirp. He had texted back! As I reached for the phone, I felt nervous. I clicked through the prompts and arrived at his text.

It's cool. No worries. Breakfast tomorrow?

My stomach flipped, in the good butterflies sort of way. He was asking me to breakfast! I instinctively looked next to me for my friend, but she wasn't there. I sighed and texted him back with a yes response, and he texted me back with a time and a place. I smiled my first genuine smile of the night. I was so excited, I could have screamed, but I didn't. I wanted to tell Leah, but she was gone. Then my head went back to her and how mad I was with her.

It took me a while to fall asleep, and when I did, it wasn't good sleep. My bad feelings kept waking me up. It made me even more angry knowing that she wasn't stewing over it like I was. The chances that she felt bad or responsible for any of it were very slim, and that thought drove me nuts.

CHAPTER SIX

The morning came, and I was disappointed to find that Leah still had not come back. I called her cell phone and left her a voicemail. I texted her twice, but she didn't respond. I took my shower and got myself ready for my first date with Blue. It could very well have been my only date with Blue. I didn't know anything about him, other than the fact that he was absolutely gorgeous. He could have lived in another state and have an equally gorgeous girlfriend for all I knew. Maybe it wasn't even a date. Maybe he wasn't thinking of it that way. Maybe he was just super friendly and trying to make buddies. Regardless, I put on makeup, did my hair really nice, and dressed fashionably, just in case.

It was a quarter to ten, and I was supposed to leave to meet him. There was still no sign of Leah. I texted her again with my plan for the morning. I wrote her a note and left it on the table as well. I didn't want her to get back to the room and not know where I was. I grabbed my purse and my car keys and headed out.

As I shut the door, the elevator chimed just down the hall. The doors opened, and Leah stepped out. She looked a mess. Her eye makeup was smudged and all over the sides of her face. She looked pale and hung over, and her hair was a rat's nest.

"Hi," I said, approaching her carefully. "How was last night?"

"Fine," she replied sheepishly. "We had fun."

"Okay. Well, I'm going to meet Blue, so..."

"Yeah?" she asked. She cracked a half smile. "That's awesome, L."

"I'm nervous," I said, laughing.

"Don't be. He'll love you." She was being sincere.

"Look, Leah, last night..."

"I know," she cut me off. "I'm sorry too. I shouldn't have put you in that position. If it makes you feel any better, it totally wasn't worth it." She laughed.

"Oh, you guys didn't?"

"No, we did. I'm saying it wasn't worth it." Her words made both of us laugh.

"Bummer," I replied. "You know those things I said..."

"I know. You're kind of right so..."

"Well, I'm sorry anyway. I shouldn't have said it," I apologized.

"L, it's fine. We're good. I'm gonna go take a shower and crawl back into bed. Wake me when you get back?"

"Sure. Need a key?"

"No, I got mine." She pulled her room key out of her pocket and waved it. "I'd say let's hug it out, but I kind of smell like a distillery, so..."

"Yeah, you do," I agreed. We laughed again. "Alright, love you. I'll be back soon."

"Have fun!" she called out to me as I went for the stairs. "L Squared!"

"L Squared!" I repeated.

The first after-fight conversation went a lot better than I had rehearsed it in my head. I felt better knowing that we'd made up. The nerves I felt over facing Leah pre hallway conversation were soon replaced by nerves about my impending meeting with Blue.

The restaurant Blue suggested was only a half block

from the hotel, but I drove anyway. I was so nervous that I was already flush, and I didn't want the heat to make it worse. I cranked the air conditioner and headed out.

Parking my car, I saw Blue standing under the awning, in front of the entrance door. He looked good. He had on a nice button up shirt and a pair of dark blue jeans. His hair was combed back, and I could swear that even from the car, I could see his eyes twinkling. He was perfect. I slyly checked myself over in the rearview mirror to make sure my makeup was still in place and my hair was behaving. Satisfied, I took a deep breath, shook out my hands, and jumped out of the car with a huge smile.

"Hey there!" he greeted me sweetly.

"Hi!" I said back. As I walked toward him, his boyish smile made me realize that he was nervous too. This was a date. His face confirmed it, and I was excited.

He opened the door for me, and we walked in. We were seated near the window, facing the main drag. The street wasn't really very busy, so there wasn't much to look at out there, but that didn't matter because I had all the scenery I needed right across from me.

"So... are you a sugar girl or a bacon and eggs kind of girl?" he asked as he glanced over his menu.

"Both, really. I love eggs and pretty much every breakfast meat you can think of, but I also love me a good waffle." I put my head down, waiting for a response. My response was honest, but I meant for it to be playful. I was really hoping he wasn't thinking, *wow, what a piggy.*

"Awesome. Me too. They have this platter thing here with bacon, sausage, eggs, hash browns, and two pancakes or a waffle. Now, I will warn you, it's a ton of food, but I think you'd like it. And, you said waffle, but I think you meant pancakes. Trust me. They're awesome!" He smiled wide, and I knew that he wasn't thinking piggy at all. So far, so good.

"Why not the waffle?"

"Don't get me wrong," he explained, "the waffles here

are good, but the pancakes are ridiculous. Once you've had the pancakes here, it's all over for you. You'll never eat pancakes anywhere else again."

I laughed and agreed to order the pancakes. The waiter came over, and we each ordered the breakfast platter. I ordered my eggs scrambled and he ordered his over easy. As he said "over easy" I kind of chuckled internally. This was easy. This was fun. I liked him.

"So," he continued. "You like BPS?"

"Yeah. They're my favorite band. You said you like them too, right?"

"Well, I kind of have to." He smiled a funny smile. "I'm sort of their road manager slash lackey."

"No way," I said in disbelief. A volt of energy surged through my body. Could I really be sitting with someone who was tight with Brick Donovan?

"Yeah, it sort of comes with the territory, I guess. It was either this or go back to school and figure out something outside the family business."

"Family business? Your family manages bands?"

"No, my family is bands," he laughed again. "Brick's my brother."

WHAT!? My head was screaming with thoughts. Excited wasn't even the word. I *was* sitting with someone close to Brick. I was sitting with his blood. I searched his face, and then I realized, that's why he looked familiar when I first saw him. He looked a lot like Brick.

"That's crazy. Seriously?" I asked, though I was pretty sure he was telling the truth.

"Yeah, but it's not all that great. My brother's cool I guess. I handle a lot of their events and stuff. You know, set up and whatnot, but I'm mostly just their errand boy. I'm sort of thinking I might go back to school to study art. Art's my real passion." He searched my face. I could feel that there was an unnatural and likely unattractive look of awe spread across it. "Need proof?" He laughed and handed me his license as well as his tour pass.

I took them into my hand and stared at them. At first I was deflated by the fact that it was a Michigan driver's license. He lived in Michigan. Then I noticed the name on his Michigan driver's license. "Beauford Donovan?" I said as I looked at the name next to probably the sexiest DMV picture I'd ever seen.

"Oh, yeah, that's my real name. People call me Blue, and thank God, 'cause I mean, Beauford? Gross, right? But it was my great-grandfather's name."

"How do you get Blue from Beauford?" I quizzed playfully.

"When we were kids, my brother couldn't quite get it right, so he called me Bluefer, and then everyone just started calling me Blue." He took a drink of his coffee and sighed. "Speaking of," he said casually, "L, like the letter; what's that about?"

I could feel myself blushing. I didn't want to explain my name, but he was so candid about his.

"Well," I started, "my name is Laverne, and I hate it, so I go by L. It's my grandma's name, but she doesn't even go by Laverne, so I guess it's cool that I don't like it either." I laughed. I was glad we had this one weird thing in common.

"Cool." He smiled.

"So, Brick and Beauford. Interesting."

"Oh, no. Melvin and Beauford. Brick's name is Melvin. His stage name is Brick." Blue smiled as if he had just made a small defeat.

"What?" I laughed a high pitched laugh. "No way!"

"Way. He's named after another distant relative. Our parents weren't very kind when choosing names."

"That's crazy. I didn't know that." I said. I realized that I was now sounding like an obsessed fan, which I was, but I didn't want Blue to know that. I really did think I knew everything about Brick Donovan, but I guess that's something they wouldn't likely print in a magazine, trying to build his image.

Our breakfast arrived. It smelled phenomenal and looked delectable. I couldn't wait to take a bite, but I didn't want to look like a hog, so I waited for him to start his first. Then, though I wanted to just shovel it all into my mouth, I took small bites of each thing. It tasted even better than it smelled. Blue was right. The pancakes were ridiculous; best I'd ever had.

"You're never gonna be able to look at pancakes the same way again, huh?" Blue said, laughing.

"Yep. You were right. These are insane." I took a bite of syrupy, pancake goodness and groaned aloud as I savored the fluffy treat.

"Told ya. So, you guys headed to Millsberg tonight? Our bus rolls out in a couple hours."

"Yeah, actually," I responded, mouth half full. I caught myself, and covered it with my hand, embarrassed. He didn't seem to notice.

"Cool. So you're like following the whole tour?"

"No," I said, carefully plotting my next sentence. I didn't want to sound like a total psycho band stalker, but he did already know that we'd been to at least two shows, and were now headed to our third. "Leah and I were just looking for some fun, girl type trip for the summer, and we heard about the Texas dates, so we decided it might be fun to, you know, just sort of follow Brick around. I mean, not follow, but, you know."

"Yeah. It's cool. You're a fan. I get it." He chuckled into his pancake.

"Yeah, well, you know. We like the music." I was trying to downplay my BPS obsession and hide the insane celebrity crush I had been harboring the last two years for his brother.

"Sure, it's good stuff. It's actually not really my thing. I'm more of a soft rock, classic kind of guy, but I appreciate my brother's talents. The band's really cool. You wanna meet 'em?" he offered, obviously not knowing how crazy this made me feel on the inside.

YES!!! I would kill to get next to Brick! I would die to touch his arm; to have his face near mine; to smell his sexy, man smell! Luckily, none of those thoughts escaped through my mouth.

"Yeah, okay," I said very calmly, though dying inside. "That might be cool." *Might be cool? AAAAH!!!!* I thought. My body was alive with electricity. I almost felt nauseas with excitement.

"Neat," he said, smiling. "I'm glad, 'cause I'd really like to see you again."

Now my excitement for Brick was turned back to Blue. He was gorgeous, super sweet, and he actually wanted to see me again.

"Neat," I said, repeating his word.

We went on with more get to know each other type conversation. I heard some about his childhood in Michigan and how he missed his mom and dad when they went on the road. I found out that he absolutely did not have a girlfriend back home or in any other part of the world. He, like me, had just gotten out of a long term relationship and was super ready to move on with his life. He'd always been a fan of abstract art and dabbled in painting and sculpting and was really considering pursuing it full time.

He gave away a few hints that he and Melvin, or Brick, didn't always get along, especially lately, but that he loved him dearly and would do anything for him. That was the only thing he really shared about Melvin, I mean Brick, and shockingly, I was okay with it and didn't ask to hear any more about him. I'm glad I didn't ask too. I didn't want Blue to think that I was using him to get next to his brother, although the fact that he was his brother was of course new information.

I told him about my teeny tiny town and what it was like growing up there. I told him about Leah, and somehow the fight we'd had the night before got worked into the discussion. I told him that I had no idea what I wanted to do with my life, but I knew I wanted something great for myself, and I was sure that I would find my path somewhere along the line while going to the community college. I told him about my interest in writing and that maybe I would explore that interest more when I got to school. It came out that I was only eighteen, and I learned that he was twenty, so neither of us could legally party, but we laughed about how we found ways to do it anyway. He told me that there was so much partying on the road, that he was just about over it and rarely drank anymore, and I told him that I could understand that, being that I was nearly fizzling out on it too. Leah and I had partied a lot over the summer, and drank way too much just in the preceding few days, and it wasn't exactly making me feel happy and energetic. I certainly wasn't quitting at that moment, but I did understand the idea of being over it.

An hour of chit chat went by in what seemed like minutes, and Blue had to get going. He was supposed to make a coffee run for the band and crew and get back to pack up again. He told me that the band was staying at the Bellinger Hotel in Millsberg and that I should call him when I got into town so we could make plans to meet up. My stomach was turning with butterflies and anticipation. This was the best first date I'd ever been on. It was really only the third first date I'd ever been on, but it definitely ranked the best.

He paid for our breakfast, and we walked out of the restaurant. We stopped just outside the doorway to say our goodbyes. He went in for a hug. I gladly accepted. His body felt so good against mine. He smelled fantastic. I breathed him in for a moment, then let go.

"Okay, great. So I'll see you tonight?" he said.

"Yeah. Tonight," I replied, smiling like a moron.

"Great." He lingered for a moment, but then he waved and turned to leave. No goodbye kiss, which was sort of refreshing. He didn't try to make any kind of move except a friendly hug. Normally, that might make me think he just wanted to be friends, but I could tell he was as into me as I was into him. It just felt right.

I couldn't wait to get back to the hotel and tell Leah all about it. Thinking of her, I stopped in the lobby and grabbed us two coffees and a muffin for her from the complimentary breakfast setup. I looked around, but I didn't see Marcus anywhere. He must have had the morning off. *Too bad,* I thought. It would have been so easy for him to get to work since he had spent the night there. I laughed to myself, but then shook it off, feeling mean for judging again.

I teetered the cups on top of each other and cradled the muffin in my arm to swipe my key card through the slot on the door. The green light flashed, and I swung the door open to find Leah, with wet hair and partial makeup done, sitting on the edge of the bed, enthralled in a talk show.

"Hey," she said. "Is that for me? You are my hero!" She eagerly jumped up and grabbed one of the coffees.

"Muffin too," I said, handing her the treat.

"Thanks! So... tell me; tell me. How was it?"

"Oh, you know," I said as I plopped down next to her. "It was magical."

She giggled and took a huge gulp from the coffee cup. She winced when the hot liquid hit her tongue, but she kept on drinking anyway.

"So," I continued, "guess what we're doing tonight?"

"Going to see BPS in Millsberg..." she said.

"No, after."

"Don't worry, I won't be bringing any guys back with us. This time, I'm all yours." She was trying to convince me that a repeat of the previous night would not occur. I was too excited about our future to even think about what had happened the night before.

"Okay, great, but what if I were to tell you that we would be starting, or possibly ending, the night with the single hottest guy in the entire universe?" I asked.

"What, like we're going home with Brick Donovan?" She laughed. I nodded my head up and down. She continued, "then I'd say, cool, and I want a unicorn to give us a ride there."

"No, seriously," I squealed, "Blue is Melvin's brother, and he said he could arrange a meeting with the band."

"Who's Melvin?" Leah cocked her head to the side.

"Brick!"

"Wait, what?"

"Brick is Melvin. Melvin is Brick. That's his real name. Look, whatever, Blue is actually on tour with Brick Party Sundae! Brick is his brother! And we are hanging out with them... tonight!"

"Shut up!" Leah screeched and hit my arm. "You're lying!" Her jaw couldn't have opened up any further.

"I'm dead serious. It's crazy, right? But he's Brick's brother for real, and you and I are going to meet up with them at some point tonight."

"Oh my god! L! Oh my god! This is crazy! You know what this means? Oh my god!" Leah was clearly losing her grip. She was reacting the way my body wanted me to when Blue told me this at the restaurant. I was definitely glad now that I had played it cool when I was with him, because this physical reaction did look really silly. She was varying between jumping up and down and dancing around the room, squealing the entire time. She finally wore herself out and then sat next to me. "L, imagine if you married Blue, you'd be like Brick's family. Then imagine, if I married Brick, we'd be like sisters!"

"Okay," I stopped her, speaking calmly. "I think you're getting a little ahead of yourself, but yes," I agreed, now joining her in her squealing, "it would be pretty perfect!" I got up, and we did a circular dance around the room, screaming and giggling like children. Nervous energy bounced back and forth between us. The adrenaline couldn't possibly have been raised any higher.

After about ten minutes of dancing around like idiots, we collected ourselves long enough to repack our stuff and get ready to leave. I did the checkout through the television so that we didn't have to hang out at the front desk.

I turned back for one last look as we were leaving. I wanted to make sure we got everything.

"What about Marcus?" I asked Leah. "You wanna leave him a note or something?"

"God, no. That's over. On to the next, my friend!" She laughed, and I laughed with her. Apparently their relationship, the whole twelve hours long that it was, had run its course.

We snuck down to the lobby, and I looked around again for Marcus. Sure he was nowhere in sight, we went to the business lounge, which was actually just one computer against the back, lobby wall, and we looked up tickets for that night's show. Luckily, there were still some left. Once again, they were way up in the back rows, but knowing that we were meeting BPS at some point that night, we didn't care where we sat for the show. I put my bank card info in as the site prompted, we printed our forty three dollars' worth of tickets, and we were ready to go. I didn't ask Leah for her money upfront; I figured we would just sit down later and figure it all out.

Millsberg was a three hour drive from Stover. We stopped off at a gas station before we began our journey to load up on gas, snacks, and beverages. I swiped my bank card through the slot, and Leah pumped the gas, while I went in to pick out some salty treats.

We were then back in the car and back on the road. Leah instructed me to the highway, and we were off on our next great adventure.

"Let's play the you're a game," Leah suggested.

"Okay," I agreed.

The *you're a game* is pretty much exactly what it sounds like. Each person is supposed to come up with a clever four word insult without actually being insulting. The rules are, no one can actually insult someone for physical or personal attributes that they are insecure about, and the goal is to make the other person laugh so hard they forget their next move and lose the game. If you take too long to come up with one, you're out, and if you repeat something someone already said, your turn doesn't count.

"You start," I said.

"Okay." Leah scrunched her face in thought. "Got one! You're a salt licking booger eater."

"You're a porcupine cuddling snot juggler!" I returned.

"You're a wool wearing wood flicker!"

"Well, you're a butt sniffing poo flinger!"

"You're a snot guzzling matchstick maker!" she said.

"Matchstick maker? That is so random!" I said, laughing.

"I know!" she shouted. "Good one, right?"

"Ah!" I put my hand up. "You can't say snot, I already used it."

"Crap! Okay, you go," she said.

"You're a... Frisbee chasing bar-fight urinator."

"A what? That's gross!" she yelled, almost choking on her giggle. This may have been my quickest and easiest defeat to date. "What does that even mean?"

"You know, you get in a fight in a bar, and you pee on 'em, so you win, or you pee yourself, and they leave you alone; either way." I explained my made-up terminology.

"Uh, yeah, I guess that'd do it!" she agreed. We both burst into laughter.

"Yeah, well," I got out in between laughs, "I win."

"No, wait," she said, "aren't bar and fight two separate words?"

"Uh, no," I made my case. "There's a hyphen. I swear." I wasn't actually sure, but it sounded accurate enough.

"Okay. You win," she admitted. "I spy?"

"Sure!"

So we played I spy, and did the alphabet game, and looked for slug bugs all the way to Millsberg. It was good, old fashioned, childish fun. We were seemingly repaired after our heated argument, and we were on our way to meet our all-time favorite band. It couldn't have been a better car ride.

CHAPTER SEVEN

We arrived in Millsberg a little after two. We had no idea where we were going to stay, but as we drove into town, the first thing we saw was a gigantic, gorgeous building with the word *Bellinger* over the entrance. That was where Blue said he was staying with the band.

"That looks nice," Leah joked. "We should stay there!"

"Yeah, right," I said. "We couldn't afford to park there, let alone spend the night. That's where BPS is staying."

"What?" Leah perked up in her seat. "L, we have to stay here then. We have to!"

"Uh, no. We can't. We don't have the million dollars."

"Don't be lame. It won't be a million. It'll probably be like a hundred at the most. Let's do it!" She was excited. It was going to be hard to talk her out of this crazy plan, but I had to. There was no way we could swing a hotel like that on our budget.

"Leah, this place doesn't have a little sign with room rates and *we've got HBO* posted out front, and I don't see any room doors on the outside, and look, no seedy, leafy pool in the middle of the parking lot. We can't afford it." I was firm. I was convincing. I definitely drove it home.

"We're staying here," she said. "We'll make it work. That's that." She sounded final. I guess I wasn't as convincing as I thought I was.

"Yeah, fine. We'll go see if they even have any rooms. I doubt they do. And I doubt we can swing it. You'll see." I made a U-turn at the light and came back around to the swanky hotel's parking lot. I found a space in the front. I didn't pull up under the awning because I noticed a guy in a red vest, just waiting to take my keys and more money.

As we walked up to the entrance, I shook my head in shame. I couldn't believe my friend was making us embarrass ourselves this way. There was no way I was staying there. No way.

"Hi," Leah said to the man at the beautiful marble counter. "We would like to make an inquiry." That was hilarious. I guess she was trying to sound uppity, but she sounded kind of silly.

"You need a room for tonight?" the gentleman asked. At Leah's nod, he continued, "alright. Let's see, I have a suite available..."

"That sounds lovely," Leah said, still sounding like a complete nerd.

"Okay, it is four hundred eighty two per night. How many nights will you be with us?"

Leah shot me a horrified look of panic. I wanted to yell *I told you so!* but I kept it in and just chuckled under my breath.

"Hmm," Leah said, "we're not really the lavish types. Do you have anything a little less... fancy." That made me want to laugh even more.

"Okay..." the man said, typing away at his keyboard, "we have a standard room with two queens for... one hundred ninety six, plus tax."

As I was trying to hold back my laughter and not make fun of my silly friend aloud, I heard a horrifying sentence escape her lips.

"We'll take it!"

WHAT? NO! I screamed inside my head.

"Leah," I whispered angrily, "tell him you're kidding."

"Shh, no, we got this. Don't worry." Leah was oddly sure of herself.

"No, I don't think we do," I replied. "Excuse me, sir, I think we need a moment."

"No, go ahead and book it. We're fine," she said, looking at me sideways. "L," she whispered, "how often do we get to say we did something this cool? Never. Come on." She was right, but there was a reason we didn't do things like this. We were broke, and somehow I was breaking a lot faster than she was. We needed to sit down and settle her debts ASAP, or I wasn't going to have a bank account left.

"Alright then," the man said. "Done. I just need a form of ID and a major credit card."

Leah patted herself down. I'd never seen her do that before. She didn't keep her cards in her pockets. In fact, neither her shirt nor the pants she was wearing at the time even had pockets.

"Shoot!" Leah said. "I left my purse in the car. L, do you mind? I'll get you back."

"Leah!" I protested.

"L, I'll get you back," she assured. I had been hearing that this whole trip, and it was starting to worry me.

"Fine," I said, giving in much too easily. I handed the man my ID, my real one this time, and my bank card, which also served as a credit card, with its shiny VISA logo in the right hand corner. Too bad my bank card was the only card I had and the only card I carried, and the money came right out of my bank account no matter which way you swiped it. I had just been steamrolled by my best friend and a snotty old man in a suit. I was not pleased.

The man then informed me that guest parking was an additional fee of twenty per night. This instantly turned me red. I could feel my face heating up as I used my internal calculator to add up how much this trip had cost me so far. My throat went dry as I realized there were too many charges to remember, and I, all of a sudden, couldn't wait to call and check my bank balance.

"Room 404. Here are your room keys, and if you will just pull around to the front and give your car to one of our attendants. They will park it for you in our garage."

"Great. Thank you," I said sourly.

Steamed, I walked out, ahead of Leah. I made an angry line toward my car.

"Oh my god, L, look!" Leah squealed from behind me. I didn't want to look, out of spite. I didn't want anything to do with her until I calmed down. "L," she kept on, "L, look!"

"What?" I yelled angrily as I spun around.

"Look!" She pointed toward the left side of the parking area, where I could see a giant, black tour bus.

It didn't say *Brick Party Sundae* on it, but I could tell it was theirs. It was black with a purple design along the side panels. It was the same design from their latest album cover art. It was beautiful. I felt the air escape me, and I could swear my heart actually skipped a beat. I couldn't believe it. I knew they were staying there, but it seemed so unreal.

"See, L, totally worth it," Leah said quietly.

"Yeah." I fought a smile, but I couldn't help it; the smile came out against my will. "Okay. Whatever." I sighed. It seemed I was once again giving into Leah's craziness.

"I knew you'd come around," she said, laughing her *I broke you down, and I win* laugh. She put her arm around my waist and kicked the back of my leg with hers.

"Hey!" I screeched. It worked. She got me laughing again. "Okay, but seriously, we have to sit down and figure out our money, like today."

"Yeah, of course. We'll get to that. Don't worry," she soothed. She smiled, showing all of her teeth. She pointed back to the bus and let out a high pitched squeal.

We laughed like kids and skipped to my car. Maybe she was right. Maybe her intuition was leading us somewhere great. I hoped for the best, and I tried to leave my fear for the worst behind. We were about to have the time of our lives. I could feel it.

As we were getting ready for our third concert, my phone chirped. I ran to it, excited to see who it was. It was a text message from Blue.

Hey L! I forgot 2 ask if U had your tix for 2night. I can get U good seats if U want them.

My face lit up. I couldn't believe this was actually happening. Was I really dating the brother of Brick Donovan, and was he really giving us a hookup?

I texted back and let him know that we were in the same hotel. I gave him our room number. He sent a note that he'd be by in a little while. My body was shaking with anticipation.

"Leah! You'll never guess. Blue says he has tickets for us... good ones!" I yelled to my friend over the noise of the blow dryer.

"What?" She shut off the dryer. "Seriously?"

"Yes!" I shouted. We linked hands and danced around in a circle, squealing, again.

"This is incredible. Who knew? Best summer ever!" Leah exclaimed.

"I know! I know!" It was like a dream. Everything felt faster and brighter than usual. I was on a cloud. I had Leah finish my makeup for me, and then I let her get back to her hair. I wanted to look perfect for my new friend, so I went through everything in my suitcase, trying to find the right outfit. Finally, I found the one. I checked myself over in the full length, closet mirror. I looked pretty great. I was definitely ready to see Blue. Even though I had just spent that morning with him, I was almost more nervous this time. Leah and I sat on the bed, flipping through channels until the knock came at the door.

"It's him!" I shrieked.

"Just breathe, L. You look fantastic," Leah said, making me feel slightly less jittery.

My heart raced as I walked to the door. I peered through the peep hole. There he was, looking oh so sexy. There was someone behind him, and I could hear them whispering to each other, but I couldn't see who it was. I swung the door open to reveal Blue's beautiful face.

"Hi," I greeted.

"Hey there," Blue said. He moved to the side, and the second person stepped forward. "Oh, hey, L, this is Milo."

It was Milo Shanks from Brick Party Sundae. He was their insanely talented lead guitarist. I felt as if my racing heart all of a sudden dropped out of my chest. I was certain that if I looked down, I might see it flopping around on the floor. I mean, I had a poster with this guy's face on it in my room.

"Hi," I said timidly. I was trying so hard not to look like a nervous super fan, but I found it hard to really focus on being cool.

"Nice to meet you," he said sweetly. Milo Shanks was sweet. Wow!

"So," Blue said, "can we?"

"Yeah, yeah, sorry," I said, finding my breath and my heartbeat. "Come on in."

They entered, and I heard Leah shuffle to her feet.

"Wow," she said, "I mean, hi." She stuck her hand out to shake Milo's. "And hello again, Blue."

"Hey," Blue said. "So, I have these VIP tickets for you girls if you want them." He reached in his front shirt pocket and pulled out two tickets. "You get front row seats and backstage passes."

"Want them?" Leah asked. "Are you kidding? Thank you! I mean, wow!"

"Yeah. Thank you," I said. "You have no idea how great this is."

"Well," Blue continued, "we have to get going, but there is an after party back here tonight, and if you want to come..."

"Yes!" Leah interrupted.

"Okay then," he said, laughing. "I was gonna say, L, if you want to come, cool, but if you just maybe want to hang out for a bit and do something else, we could skip it."

Leah squeezed my elbow. Clearly, we were going to the party.

"Well," I said, half tempted to take him up on his quiet night offer. Then again, who was I kidding? I wanted to meet Brick. "We could stop by the party for a bit and see what happens." That was the perfect solution, I thought. We go to the party, meet the rest of the band, then Blue and I would still get to spend time together, and if we wanted to, we could always leave.

"Sure. Sounds good. Uh, so, just come back to your room after the show, and I'll come grab you guys when we get back." Blue smiled wide. "I mean, I'll see you at the show, but you know, always good to have a plan." He actually sounded nervous. Did I really make this incredible guy nervous?

"Okay," I agreed.

He kissed me on the cheek. As he leaned in, I could smell his intoxicating cologne. It gave me goose bumps.

"Alright. See you later. Bye," Blue said.

"Bye," Milo echoed and waved.

Leah and I waved back and watched them leave the room. Then the squealing commenced once again. We jumped up and down and did the L Squared handshake a couple times. Out of breath, we finally wound ourselves down long enough to come up with a tentative plan for the evening. It was an hour and a half before show time.

"Your boyfriend is so cool!" Leah shouted.

"He's not my boyfriend. But yes, he is pretty fantastic." I smiled, imagining how things might unfold for Blue and I in the future. I knew better than to get ahead of myself, but I couldn't help the daydreaming.

"So, what do we do with the crappy tickets we bought

earlier?" Leah asked.

"I don't know..." I said, thinking.

"I know! We can scalp them!" She was obviously excited by the idea.

"Uh, no. That's a terrible idea." I was less enthused.

"Come on, L. We go a little early, make some extra cash; it'll be awesome!" Leah rationalized.

"No. Not awesome. Bad. It's a bad idea. Speaking of money, we really should...."

"Hey!" Leah cut me off. "Let's go down stairs and give the crap tickets to some unsuspecting strangers. It'll be fun... like our own little hidden camera, surprise giveaway show! It'll be our good deed for the day. We'll pay it forward or whatever."

"Yeah. Okay!" I liked the idea.

We grabbed our room keys and the print out tickets we'd purchased online and made our way downstairs to the lobby. The lobby was surprisingly crowded. Apparently, as we found out later, there was some kind of medical convention in town, and everyone was just arriving for check in. I saw a girl, who looked to be Becca's age, sitting alone on the large green couch in the sitting area. She was clearly waiting for her parents to check in. I walked toward the girl and took a seat next to her.

"Hi," I said.

"Uh, hi," she said back.

"So, you here with your mom and dad?" I asked her.

"My mom. She's over there..." she said, pointing toward the counter.

"You like Brick Party Sundae?" I asked her.

"I love Brick Party Sundae!" she replied.

"Do you think your mom would let you go to the concert tonight?"

"With you?" She looked confused and a little nervous. I laughed. I must've been coming across a little weird. I didn't care though. I was too happy to care.

"No, with your mom. We have two extra tickets, and we're looking for someone to take them off our hands."

"No way!" she shouted. "How much?" Her face dropped a little.

"No, no. Free. We just happened to come across better seats, so we're giving these away."

"Really?" she asked apprehensively.

"Really," I said.

"Well, I guess I have to ask my mom."

"Ask me what?" A pretty woman in a suit dress came over to us.

"These girls just offered me free tickets to Brick Party Sundae tonight. Can we go?"

"Uh..." Her mother hesitated.

"Here," I said. I showed the mom the tickets. "They're all yours if you want them."

"Yeah. Why not? I forced you all the way out here for my convention. Might as well have some fun," the mom gave in. We did it. We made someone's night. It felt good.

"Awesome!" the girl shouted. "Thanks, Mom! And thank you..."

"L. I'm L, and this is Leah," I introduced us. Leah waved.

"Thanks, L!" she yelled. She was so excited.

"No prob. Have fun!" I said. With that, my friend and I were on our way back to the room.

An hour later, we were walking the three blocks to the venue. We skipped and danced and giggled the entire way. We hadn't had a thing to drink, yet we were drunk on happiness. This was shaping up to be the best night of the entire summer.

When we got to the entrance, we were more than happy to give over our tickets and flash our passes. Once inside the gate, a large guard took us down to the VIP section in the front row. He asked if we wanted to go backstage now or after, and we, of course, unable to wait, told him that we wanted to go right then.

He escorted us to the backstage area, where another security guard inspected our passes. As he was looking them over, Blue appeared from behind a curtain.

"Hey, you two!" Blue said. "It's cool; they're with me." He waved us over to him.

I loved how he said *they're with me*. I felt so important and, let's face it, cool. It felt like we were really something.

"Brick and the guys are, uh, warming up, so you can't meet them now, but you'll see them later at the suite party," Blue told us.

"Cool," I said, trying to sound casual and unconcerned. I was dying inside. This was the craziest, most noteworthy thing I'd ever done.

"I'll give you a quick tour, and then you guys can grab a drink and take a seat. Wish I could sit with you, but I have to hang around back here." Blue grabbed my hand, sending electricity up my spine. Our hands fit perfectly together.

"Okay," I said, having not even really heard what he said. Once he touched me, it all went fuzzy.

We walked around, careful not to trip over the cables and frantic people. It was pure mayhem back there, but Blue seemed really calm and collected. The tour was really quick. Though I'm sure he was, it didn't feel like he was trying to rush us. He was totally in control.

"Hey, Blue, do you know which way Meryl went? I need help with this stupid zipper," a woman's voice said from behind.

I turned around to see it was Melanie Rave from Mel Says Go. She was stunning up close. She almost looked fake, she was so pretty. Her purple hair glowed in the florescent lights.

"Hi," she said, addressing me and Leah. "I'm sorry, but I really need to find her. This thing won't budge. I'm kind of stuck."

"Yeah, let me get her on the walkie." Blue grabbed the

walkie talkie from his belt and made a request for Meryl's location. She came over the walkie, saying that she'd meet Mel in her dressing room. This was the coolest thing I'd ever seen, backstage band madness in action.

"Thank you," Mel said sweetly. Then, she was gone.

"Sorry about that. For some reason, Meryl always disappears at the worst times." Blue laughed.

"It's okay," I said. I looked at Leah, who simply smiled. She had no words.

"Alright, so here are some wine coolers. I hope that's okay, but that's really all we have back over here. I can get you some beer vouchers for the vendors," Blue offered.

"No, this is fine. Thank you," I said.

Blue handed us two each. He took one back from me so that he could hold my hand again. He escorted us back through all the madness to our side of the stage. He walked us down to our seats and handed me the second wine cooler.

"Well," he said, "enjoy the show. I will see you back at the hotel after." He kissed me on the cheek. I nodded, and he took off in a hurry backstage.

"So I guess Mel Says Go is opening again," I said, laughing.

"Oh... my.... god..." Leah said slowly. "Did that seriously just happen?"

"Yeah, I think it did."

"Wow," Leah said. She popped the top off one of her coolers and took a huge drink. "Just, wow."

"I know." I couldn't believe it either.

Just as the lights went crazy and the emcee came out to introduce the band, I saw Blue poke his head out from the side of the stage. He winked at me and then disappeared into the background. I smiled and giggled to myself.

Mel Says Go was even better than the first two times we'd seen them. When Mel got up on stage, she scanned the audience, and I could swear she winked at me. It was awesome. Their set lasted somewhere around forty-five blissful minutes. Leah and I danced and cheered until our voices felt weak.

Then, it was time for Brick Party Sundae. A new wave of adrenaline jolted through my body and got my heart pumping even faster. I screamed with excitement. Leah squeezed my hand. She wanted to scream too, I could tell, but the sound just wouldn't come out. She was shaking with anticipation.

The eight minutes from the time Mel Says Go left the stage and BPS was announced, seemed like an eternity. Finally, the emcee came back and announced what we all wanted to hear.

Milo came out and waved to the crowd. He picked up his guitar and settled in for the set. Sam D, the drummer, and Sam G, the bassist, took to their positions. There was a hush over the crowd, at least that's how I remember it. Our breath stopped as we waited for Brick to appear at the microphone. Again, that's just how it felt; I may have been the only one holding their breath; I can't be sure.

Then, I saw a foot step out from the side of the stage. A leg followed, then a hip, and then a body. It was Brick, and he was so close to us. He was elevated just a few feet above us on stage, and he looked like an angel. His skin was illuminated by the stage lights. His hair shined in the glow. He almost sparkled. He was so beautiful, and we were so close, we could almost touch him. My hand instinctively reached up and out, toward the stage. He was right there! My muscles tingled. My legs felt like jelly. It was insane.

He got to the microphone, and they began. It was the same set we'd seen them do twice before, but it seemed different. It was more perfect than the other times. It had some kind of special meaning. It felt like this time the songs really were just for us. The crowd behind us became nonexistent. Leah and I immersed ourselves in the moment, and everyone else faded away. During the second song, Brick glanced down at us, and he smiled a little knowing smile.

Leah clutched my arm and cheered. She was finally making noise again.

Then, the biggest moment of the entire concert came during the sixth song. It was their love song, *Love Meets Love,* from their album of the same title. Brick came toward the edge of the stage. He was right in front of us, and he was looking right at me. He knelt down and held out his beautiful, silken hand.

"Oh my god! Oh my god!" I heard Leah say.

The hand was for me. I was supposed to touch it. I ran to him and put my hand in his. He smiled as he sang the next verse, all the while holding my hand. He finished the line just before the instrumental bridge, he kissed my hand softly, he winked at me, and then he let go. Brick Donovan had kissed my hand! *MY* hand! I pulled my hand back gently, cradling it inside my other hand in pure disbelief.

I walked backwards, very slowly, and took my place next to Leah.

"L!" she shouted over the music. "You are such a beotch! Lucky!" She smiled and laughed as she feigned excitement for me, but I could see her eyes turning green. I didn't really take it into consideration much at the time. I didn't really have the capacity to think about anything at the moment. I had just had physical contact with Brick Donovan, the most gorgeous man in the universe. He sang to me. That's right, me! And everyone there was a witness to it. I was floating on air. Nothing could bring me down.

The rest of the concert went on, just as it had the nights before. We danced and sang along joyously to every song. It was incredible, and we didn't want it to end, but eventually, sadly, it did.

As the lights came up over the seats, and the crowd started to filter out, I saw Blue coming across the stage toward me. He was so cute in his band t-shirt and cargo pants.

"So," he said, "what did you guys think? You have fun?"

"Yes!" I shouted over the ringing in my ears. It was the most fun I'd had the entire trip.

"Yeah, it was pretty cool," Leah said. "Thank you for the hookup."

"Yes," I added, "thank you. It was amazing."

"No problem. I'm glad you girls had fun," he said sweetly. "So, I'll come by your room in a little bit, and we'll head over to the suite, yeah?"

"Yes!" Leah responded eagerly. "We'll be there!"

"Okay, great," he said, glancing quickly behind him. "Well there's tons to do, so I have to get, but I'll see you ladies in a bit."

"Okay," I said, smiling. He was adorable. I couldn't help but smile around him.

"Oh and by the way," he noted, "I saw that. Trying to make me jealous?" He laughed. He was jokingly referring to my having held his brother's hand.

"Oh," I said, laughing and matching his jovial tone, "it was nothing." I said it was nothing, but in my super fan, crazed brain, it was everything. I really liked Blue though, and realistically, the hand holding thing was just part of the show. I'd seen him do it twice before at the other shows with two other random girls, so though it was fun to think I may have shared an actual romantic moment with Brick, and though it made me feel incredibly special, I knew it didn't mean anything whatsoever to the sexy Brick Donovan. His brother, on the other hand, that seemed like it was shaping into something real.

"Good. Glad to hear that," Blue said. "Okay, see you later." He waved and jumped up to run backstage.

"L," Leah said, nudging my arm, "we should get going."

"Yeah," I agreed. "Let's go."

We took off for the exit and made our way back to our insanely expensive hotel.

CHAPTER EIGHT

Back in our luxury room, which by the way wasn't all that great for two hundred bucks, we spruced up our makeup and redid our hair in preparation for the after party.

"After party," I said to Leah. "Can you believe we are going to a real live after party? I mean, how crazy is this?"

"I know, right? Insane," she said. "Can I have a couple bucks for the machine? I'm crazy hungry."

"Why don't you go to the car and grab some of our home snacks? I think we still have some crackers and a bunch of fruit snacks." I was trying to think of what we had left in the car from our home pantry invasions. I didn't really want to spend the money on vending.

"No," Leah replied, "I'm not really in the mood for fruit snacks. I need something more substantial, you know? I just need a couple ones."

"Uh, sure." I was hesitant. I had paid for nearly everything so far, and Leah hadn't paid me back for any of it. She had yet to pay me for her share of the rooms for this night and the night before, and she hadn't paid me back for the tickets I'd bought online earlier that day either. She hadn't even offered to pay for gas. Nevertheless, I reached inside my purse and grabbed three bills for her. "Bring me something salty," I said.

"Sure!" She was out the door.

While she was gone, I took the time alone to call my bank from my cell phone to check my balance. I nervously went through the prompts. I tried to add it all up in my head real quick so that it wouldn't be so much of a devastating shock when my balance was revealed by the robotic voice in the receiver. I added three tanks of gas, plus the tickets, plus the rooms, and I figured it might be okay. I should still have at least four hundred left.

The robot finally came back and said, "Balance is one hundred eighty two dollars and fifteen cents."

WHAT? Thoughts flooded my brain and bad feelings invaded my body. I started to panic. I hit the buttons to get myself back the main menu and selected to hear my last ten transactions. I listened intently. There had to be some mistake somewhere. They rolled out one by one, and I heard no mistakes. All I heard were charges I expected and some I had forgotten. There were the gas stations, the hotels, the online ticketing, the cafe charges from our time in Hadley, and there were a few ATM withdrawals, which on their own totaled almost two hundred dollars. It was crazy, but it was right. I hadn't paid enough attention to my spending, and I was in trouble. I hung up the phone and then thought back to my cash. Where had I been spending that? I knew we'd spent some money on liquor, then there were the overpriced, scalped tickets, the beer and stuff we bought at the Hadley County Fair, a few drive-thru trips, and then the cab rides in Stover that I'd paid for. I checked my purse, desperately looking for cash, hoping and praying that there would be a giant stash of unspent money, but there wasn't. I found thirty two dollars, some quarters, and a bunch of pennies.

I had done it. I had spent almost five hundred dollars in only three days. Then a thought occurred to me. Leah. It would be fine because Leah owed me half of it. She said she'd make good, and I knew she would. I just needed to put it on paper for her.

I sat down and started writing down all the things I'd paid for that we were supposed to be in on fifty-fifty. Her total was just over two hundred fifty dollars. It was fine. She would give me that money to replenish my account, and I'd still have enough for tuition. Then another horror manifested. Sure, she could pay me back, but then what? I literally would have enough for a gas tank home and my tuition. I couldn't help but wonder why this was turning out to be so much more expensive than we'd planned, but then I realized, it was because we didn't really plan any of it. We were just flying by the seat of our pants.

I suddenly felt very stupid and very small. Here, we thought we were these grown-ups who could do anything they wanted, but in reality, we had no idea what we were doing, and it felt really awful to reach that realization.

I was on the verge of tears when Leah appeared back in the room.

"Oh my god, Leah!" I said as she came toward me. "I just checked my bank account, and it's bottoming out fast. I kind of need you to settle now if that's cool."

"Uh, yeah," Leah said as she opened her pretzel bag. "I have like eighty bucks in cash. I can give you like half of that now."

"Well, see, it's kind of a lot more than forty bucks, Leah. Here, I wrote it all down. Your half is more like two fifty." I handed her the paper I'd worked out.

"Wow," she said, looking over the numbers. "I see. How did we go through it so fast?"

"I don't know. I guess we weren't as careful as we thought." I shrugged.

"Wow. Okay. Well, how about I get you that forty now, and we work the rest out later," she suggested.

"Later when? I kind of need that money. I thought you said you had a few hundred saved up or whatever."

"Yeah, well," she continued, "I may have accidentally exaggerated that a little. I guess I don't have as much as I thought I did. But don't worry; I'll get it to you when we get home. No big."

"No big?" I asked angrily. "How is that no big? It's a huge big!"

"What?" she said, laughing at my terminology.

"You know what I mean, Leah. This isn't okay. I don't have enough for tuition now. This is terrible. What am I supposed to do?"

"Take less classes," she said playfully.

"It's not funny, Leah!" I yelled. I couldn't believe how flippant she was being. "What are you gonna do? How are you gonna afford classes if you can't even pay me back for this trip?"

"Yeah, I was gonna tell you..." Leah said. "I'm not really planning on going in the fall. I was thinking I might take some time off and maybe start in during the spring semester or maybe even the next fall. I don't really know. You know me, L. School's not really my thing. I'm kind of burnt out."

"Burnt out? You don't do anything!" I shouted, even more angry than before. "You don't have a job or any other responsibilities to speak of. What exactly will you be doing with your time, genius?"

"I don't know. God!" She was getting mad now. "Maybe I'll get a job. I hear there's an opening at Marnie's." She smiled.

"Oh, very funny. I only left that job to come on this stupid trip with you. You talked me into this whole thing, and now you can't even hold up your end. And you're not going to school? That was our plan all along. We picked out our course plans together! It's like I don't even know you."

She glanced back at the paper, looking for something else to say.

"Oh," she said, pointing to one of the numbers, "I'm not paying for this one. I didn't even spend the night in that room last night. That one's all you." She pointed at the mark for the night before in Stover.

"You used the room when you came back in the morning, didn't you?"

"Barely. I slept for like an hour and took a shower. Big deal," she argued.

"The only reason you didn't spend the night in it is because you were busy handing yourself out to the first available guy who looked your direction. You agreed to stay there. It's not my problem you were out being a super skank. Maybe that's what you could do with yourself now that you'll have all this free time. You are good at it; you should start charging. Perhaps you'll be able to pay me back after, oh a month or so of doing what you do best."

"Shut up!" she yelled. Her face was bright red. I guess I hit below the belt on that one. Maybe it was unnecessary, and maybe it was mean, but I was really angry, and it was sort of true.

"Whatever, you don't want to pay for that one, fine, but I want the rest of my money," I said. I was so mad that it had boiled down to this. I had to bully my best friend for her share of what was supposed to be the best road trip of all time. I was angry, and let down, and a little embarrassed too. I couldn't believe it had come to this. This was only our second serious fight ever, the first one having been just the night before, and I couldn't believe it was happening at all.

"You'll get your money," she said sternly and bitterly. "After that though, I think we're done."

Had she really just ended our friendship because I asked her to pay her fair share? Unbelievable. Maybe I really didn't know her. Or maybe it was just that I didn't know her in this particular situation. We had never taken a trip together before, and we had never had to split this kind of expense, so I guess I'd just never seen what she was like in this kind of position. I didn't like it, and she apparently didn't like me in this situation either. I searched my brain for a way to mend the giant canyon of a rift we'd just created, but I was so mad, my efforts were pretty small. Luckily, Leah was willing to try a tiny bit harder than I was.

"Look, L, I don't wanna fight. I'm sorry. You're right. I've been irresponsible. But I swear, when we get home, I'll figure out a way to get you that money. You'll get to school. Don't worry." She sounded sincere. Of course, in that situation, she would have had to be the one to make the first apology.

"Well," I started, unwilling to fully give up the argument but knowing it had to be put aside for the time being. "Okay. I'm sorry for the whole prostitute thing. You're not a hooker." That was about the only thing I could apologize for. I definitely meant the rest of it.

"Thanks." She smiled halfheartedly. "L Squared?" she asked, holding up her right hand in an L shape.

"L Squared". I repeated, holding my hand in an L shape to hers. I smiled, but in my head, I was still fuming mad. I couldn't believe how horrible she'd made this trip. I was so angry that she was just now telling me that she had no real intention of going to school with me, and I was baffled by the fact that she never had enough money for the trip in the first place. Did she really think I wouldn't notice how broke I was by the time we were done? And how were we supposed to make it another five days on my bank account alone? It was impossible.

For the sake of the night though, I decided to make an effort to feign a mended friendship. Blue would be there any minute, and I knew that no matter what, the looming possibility of meeting BPS was the only thing Leah would really be able to focus on, so we weren't going to get anywhere talking about it anymore that night. Besides, I figured we both needed some time to really think and sort it out before we ended up in a great big argument again. After all, we were best friends. We should have been able to work through anything. I hoped that maybe the next day we could just sit and talk about it like rational, civilized humans. I was frustrated, but this was L Squared. L Squared was tight.

There was no breaking up L Squared.

We hugged briefly and laughed and sighed a deep sigh together.

"We'll work it out, L. You'll see," she said.

"I know," I said, really believing we would.

Just then, there was a tap at the door.

"It's your boyfriend!" Leah teased, winking at me.

"Shh," I shushed her playfully. I pranced to the door and looked through the peep hole. It was Blue. His hair was wet like he'd just showered, and he was wearing different clothes. Instead of a band shirt, he was wearing a nice looking, green, pinstriped shirt, and in lieu of cargo pants, he was wearing dark wash jeans.

I opened the door to find him standing there alone, no band members in tow.

"Hello, pretty lady," he said as he went in for a hug.

As I hugged him, I felt the door try to close on my hip. It kind of hurt, but I didn't really care. I breathed in his scent.

"Come in," I said.

He and Leah said their greetings to each other.

"You ready to go up?" He asked.

"We sure are!" Leah said.

"Okay, great. Let's go then," Blue said, motioning toward the door.

I grabbed the key cards, handing one to Leah. I put my card in my back pocket and followed Blue out the door and to the elevator. He swiped his key card in the side and hit the button for the penthouse floor. My heart skipped a beat again. We were actually headed to the penthouse suite. My insides were screaming. I glanced nervously at my friend, who, I could see, was also going crazy on the inside. She was acting pretty calm and collected, but I could see the nerves on her face.

"Wow," she said as she exhaled, "I could sure use a drink."

"Oh, well, we have plenty to drink upstairs." Blue

grabbed my hand. I gladly let our fingers intertwine as the elevator doors opened to reveal a much fancier carpet pattern than the one on our floor and pretty gold fixtures on the walls.

He led us to the suite door. Next to the door was a very large, building of a man, dressed in all black. I could guess that he was the security, so there was no need to ask. I smiled at him. Without changing his stoic expression, he nodded to acknowledge me. Just down the hall I noticed two girls, likely close in age to Leah and I, stumbling around and laughing. They were scantily clad, and I instantly felt like judging them in my head, but at the same time, I felt slightly intimidated by their overdone faces and tiny skirts. I looked to Leah, who was scowling in their direction. I could see her hackles go up. She obviously felt the same, maybe even more so.

The anticipation built as I watched Blue swipe his key card into the card reader on the large double-doors. It was almost as if he were moving in slow motion. The light flashed green, and the door was opened, and we were moving inside. Once inside the large living room area, I searched the room from wall to wall with my eyes, scanning each person for a familiar face. I saw Sam D and Sam G in the corner by the wet bar, popping tops off of beer bottles for a small mix of people, then I noticed Milo Shanks sitting alone in a chair, smoking a cigarette, speaking to no one, and then, two bodies cleared away from the front of the couch, and I saw Brick Donovan, sitting in the middle of the couch, a ridiculously good looking girl on each side of him with one on each side of them. He looked like some kind of royalty among his beautiful harem. All of the girls were sitting, legs crossed toward him, listening intently to whatever it was he was talking about.

"Come on," Blue said, "I want you to meet my brother."

I went with him, silently. It felt more and more like a dream as the seconds passed. Leah followed quietly behind me.

"Hey, Brick," Blue said, interrupting the beautiful man, "this is the girl I was telling you about. This is L."

"L," Brick said. "Right. Nice to meet you." He extended his perfect, silken hand to me. It was the same hand I had held just a short time before. I placed my hand inside it and felt his warmth. I could envision myself melting into him, becoming one with his soul, but my vision was cut short when Blue continued.

"And this is Leah," Blue introduced my friend.

Brick instantly let go of my hand to greet Leah.

"Pleasure," he said. One simple word, the perfect word. Pleasure was right.

"Hi," Leah said nervously. "I love you. I mean your music. I love your music." She recovered nicely from the proclamation of love.

"Thank you. I appreciate that," Brick said. His eyes sparkled in the warm glow of the room. "Hang out. Have a drink. Bar's over there," Brick said, pointing toward the Sams.

"Sure," Leah said. "Thanks."

The three of us turned and walked toward the bar. I could read Leah's mind. I knew that she wanted so badly to squeal or jig or something to let out this crazy nervous energy she had. I knew that because that's how I felt, and we were generally on the same page when it came to this sort of thing. I glanced at her coyly, and she glanced to me and gave a slight smile, trying her best to keep her nerves in check.

We reached the bar, and I realized I was now literally touching elbows with Sam D. He went to turn and jabbed me in the bicep.

"Oh my god!" he shouted as he jumped sideways to avoid the splash back from his beer. "I am so sorry," he apologized.

Sam D had just elbowed me and apologized. I knew that I would likely tell people this story for years and years to come.

"It's okay," I said casually, grabbing his arm. "No harm done." I smiled. *No harm done.* I was being so calm, so cool. I felt for a moment like I was really fitting in there. I felt like I actually belonged at this swanky party with these super important people. It was fantastic.

"Here," he said, laughing, "drinks on me." He went toward the bar and placed his beer on the surface of the counter. "What will it be, ladies?"

"Uh..." I looked around at all the options. They had every imaginable label and some I had never even heard of on display on top of, under, and behind the bar.

"Okay," he said, picking up on the fact that this decision was clearly overwhelming. "How about rum and cola? They're easy, so I rarely mess those up, and you really can't go wrong with rum."

I glanced at the rum bottle next to his hand. It was brand new, unopened, and calling out my name.

"Sure!" I agreed excitedly.

"Rum it is. And for you?" Sam D asked Leah.

"Same," Leah said.

"You girls are easy!" he said. "Wait, I mean, well you know..." He blushed at his blunder. A rock star had just gotten nervous in front of us and turned red. Was this for real? It was. He was bright red and giggling to himself like a little kid.

"You have no idea how easy," Leah said.

"Leah!" I scolded, elbowing her in the ribs.

"Ouch! L, I was joking. Obviously." She looked at me and laughed.

The problem was, it kind of embarrassed me, and I knew that, unfortunately, she likely wasn't joking. Then I, in my usual nature, felt guilty for having jumped to that conclusion, so I sheepishly apologized and laughed along with the both of them so as to make light of it and move forward.

"Alright. Here you go!" He handed us each a cup. "Want something, Blue?"

"Just a beer. I'll get it," Blue responded as he went into the mini fridge and pulled out an import.

Sam D handed Blue a bottle opener, and the two shared a laugh about something that had happened earlier in the night. I smiled as I half listened to their story. The rest of me was busy scoping out the rest of the party. It was a pretty large crowd for a hotel suite. Granted, the suite itself was kind of huge, but I was sort of surprised to see that many people there. There was a mix of men and women there. All of them were our age or older, and everyone was attractive. It felt very posh and very exclusive. I still couldn't get over the fact that we were actually there with all these gorgeous and interesting people.

Blue kept putting his arm around me, which made me feel good. I felt like we were a couple, and he wanted people to know it. I didn't have to worry about the tiny skirted competition. At some point during the laughter and drinking, I noticed the large man from outside the door had come in to join the festivities. He was all talk and laughs, not at all like I would have expected him to be. His name was Morris. He was actually very sweet and funny. He was from Brick's and Blue's hometown. They'd known him since they were kids. Apparently, he was once a very talented football player and was well on his way to playing pro ball when a car accident severely injured him and took out his knee. He was all in one piece and had healed well but not well enough to keep playing. He seemed to be full of interesting stories, but we didn't get to hear too many of them, as we were eventually waved over by Brick to come sit with him.

We were all about three drinks in and feeling pretty great. Brick seemed to be feeling no pain as well. He was definitely further gone than we were. He was sitting down, but for some reason, he still seemed to not be able to control his swaying. He was happy though; all smiles and laughs.

Blue and I sat directly next to Brick on the couch. Two of the girls had gone into the bathroom and left an open space. Leah sat straight across from us in a chair.

"What was your name again, angel?" he asked me.

"L. Like the letter," I said cutely.

"Oh. Can I just call you angel? You look like an angel," he said. "Hey," he continued, "L... ange-L, ha! Get it? It's perfect." He laughed to himself and put his hand on top of mine.

"Okay," I agreed, though I wasn't really sure why he couldn't just call me by my actual name. One syllable seemed easier than two, but I wasn't about to argue with the most beautiful creature on the planet.

"Watch the angel stuff," Blue said, batting Brick's hand away. Blue laughed and grabbed my hand.

"Right, right, sorry, bro," Brick said, chuckling. "And what about you?" He looked to Leah.

"Me?" she asked. "I'm Leah."

"Yes, Leah. That's right. I like that name. That's a beautiful name," he said. He went to stand but stumbled backwards onto the couch. "The gravity in this place is unbelievable," he joked. "I need another drink. Sam!" he yelled toward the bar. "Sam! Bring me something!" He sounded demanding.

"Maybe you should lay off for a little bit; have something to eat," Blue suggested.

"Maybe you should just go to Hell," Brick snapped back.

Blue hung his head and fell quiet. I looked at him, and he just looked back with an apologetic face.

"Sam! Where's my drink, Sam?" Brick kept yelling for Sam, which Sam I'm not sure, but Sam G finally brought him a drink to quiet him down. Sam G promptly left and went about his business over by the bar. They didn't quite seem like the tight-knit family they'd painted themselves to be in all the articles I'd read. There was some obvious, deep seeded tension, and it sort of seemed that they didn't even like each other. I looked around. Brick was here with us, drunk as drunk can be, barking, Milo was still in his chair, still smoking, and still alone, and the Sams were by the bar, talking up some random new comers. They seemed like the only ones who could actually maybe stand each other.

"So," Brick slurred, "you girls wanna party serious?"

"Uh," I said, "I'm not sure I..."

"No," Blue said. "They're good."

"I wasn't talking to you!" Brick shouted over me at his brother. "Anyway, how 'bout it, angel?" Brick asked me. As I looked at him, I realized he was trying to look me in the eye, but he couldn't quite focus. His eyes were glazed over, and he was almost staring past me. This wasn't the romantic, wonderful person I'd imagined for all these years. This guy was a drunk and kind of a jerk.

"Uh, I'm still not really sure what you mean, but I'm fine right here." I looked to Blue, who smiled at me and grabbed my hand tighter.

"Sorry," Blue whispered.

"Aw," Brick said, making a pout, "come on, angel." He put his hand on my leg and it started traveling upward.

"No. Really," I said, removing his paw and placing it back in his own lap. "I'm good."

"How about you then, uh... Leah? Yeah, Leah. You wanna party serious? Huh?" He looked drunkenly to my friend.

I looked to her and nodded toward the door, trying to get her to acknowledge that I was motioning for us to leave, but she just winced at me to quit and ignored my gesture.

"Sure. What did you have in mind?" Leah said flirtatiously.

"Well, come on over here, angel, and I'll tell you." Brick shooed away the girl on the other side of him to make room for Leah. He patted the couch cushion and motioned for Leah to join him.

She hopped on over and took her place at his side.

"It just so happens that the room over there is mine," he said sloppily, pointing toward the bedroom to the right. "It's all mine, angel, and after we do this, it can be ours. All ours... and possibly hers too." He laughed arrogantly and winked at another girl across the room. "We'll see where it takes us."

He pulled a tiny plastic bag from his shirt pocket. I'd never done drugs before, but I'd seen enough movies to guess what it was.

"You ever done blow, my love?" he asked Leah.

"Not really," she said nervously.

"Not really?" I cut in. "Not ever! And she's not about to start now. Come on, Leah. We're out!" I jumped up and waited for Leah to jump up angrily too, but she didn't budge. Blue jumped up with me, ready to bolt on my cue.

"L, come on. It can't hurt to just try a little," Leah said, looking me straight in the face.

"Leah, no. We're leaving. Let's go!" I demanded.

"No. You go. I'm staying." Leah just sat there. She was being stupid. I was so angry. I wanted to wrap my fingers in her hair and pull her out.

"See, angel," Brick said to me, "it's all good. Come be one with us. Sit. Sit."

"No. Seriously. Leah, we're going." I stomped the ground with my right foot, but it didn't seem to have the desired effect.

"L, it's no big deal. Just this one time." I could see how nervous she was, but for some reason, she really wanted to stay.

"Leah, I have heard enough *it's no big deals* from your mouth to last a lifetime. This is a big deal, and you're not doing it. We are leaving!" I stomped the ground again but to no avail. Blue was standing firmly beside me.

"Brick, come on. Put that away. She's not into it," Blue said, urging his brother to put the drugs away.

"Is that true, angel? You're not into it?" Brick asked

Leah. He put his hand on her leg. "You gonna let them tell you what you're into?"

She looked at him and then looked to me with a strange look of determination I'd never seen on her face before.

"No, I'm not," she answered. "I'm staying. You wanna go? Then go. I don't need a babysitter."

"Well, alright! Looks like it's on! Rock and roll!" Brick said, delighted. Instead of the beautiful being I had once seen, he was now the most hideous creature I had ever had the displeasure of making acquaintance with.

"Leah," I urged once more, "I am leaving. I really wish you would come with me."

She didn't answer. She just shook her head and stayed seated next to the BPS monster.

"Fine," I said. I started for the door, Blue still beside me.

I nodded to the Sams as we left, but they didn't acknowledge us. They were busy talking up the two young girls I'd seen earlier in the hallway. I suddenly wondered just how young the girls were. They looked close to our age, but we were barely eighteen. I wondered if those girls even belonged there. The entire suite now felt tainted and disgusting.

We reached the warm glow of the hallway and the large, suite doors slammed behind us. I leaned against the wall next to the doors and slid down it to the floor. Blue knelt down next to me.

"I'm so sorry, L," he said as he played with my hand. "I asked him before you guys came up if he could just this once not be a total jerk. I guess there's no such thing as small favors when it comes to my brother. I'm sorry Leah's getting mixed up in this."

"Yeah, well she's a big girl," I said, though I didn't believe it. This whole trip she'd been so irresponsible, so reckless, and now she was doing the ultimate wrong we swore we'd never do. I started to well up. I was so frustrated, so mad, and so terribly hurt and disappointed. I really didn't know her like I thought I did.

"Hey, hey!" Blue consoled, seeing my tears. "It's okay. Maybe Brick will change his mind."

"Really? Does he do that?"

"No. He doesn't, but maybe this one time... Yeah, okay, probably not. He does whatever he wants. I'm so sick of it!" Blue yelled.

"Have you ever?" I asked.

"Me? Coke? No way! It rots your mind. Literally. I swear my brother has gotten meaner and dumber with every snort. I've tried to get him to quit, but he won't listen to me." Blue hung his head. "This is a lot of why I want out. I can't wait 'til this tour is over next week. I really just want to go back home and finish school. You know?"

"Yeah," I said, "I know. You should. That's exactly what you should do. Don't let Brick, or I mean Melvin, hold you back. Do what you need to do for you. It's not his life. It's yours."

"You know, I could say the same to you right now," Blue noted.

"Yeah, well, Leah's not a lost cause. At least I don't think she is. This is the first time I've really seen her act like this. It's crazy. I feel like I need to protect her," I admitted.

"Well, that's not your job. You really tried back there. It's up to her now, L. You can't worry about her all the time. Just worry about you." He lifted my chin with his hand. He looked into my teary eyes and smiled. And then, we kissed. It was soft and sweet and perfect. I wish our first kiss had been under better circumstances, but it still seemed magical, and it still managed to send sparks right through me.

I smiled at him as we pulled away. It was over. That was going to be the extent of our kissing, and it seemed like enough; one magic moment to hang onto even though the rest of the night seemed otherwise contaminated. We just sat there in that hallway for about half an hour. He let me be silent. He knew I needed some time to collect myself. After a while, I told him I was okay and that I should probably just get to bed.

"Come on," he said kindly, "I'll walk you back."

We got up, and he put his arm around me. I let my body relax into his side. I seemed to fit there perfectly. We stepped inside the elevator, and he held me close as the floors ticked away. We reached my floor, and he walked me to my door. I pulled my key card out of my back pocket but hesitated to swipe it through.

"You know," I said, turning back to him, "I've had a really great time getting to know you."

"Me too," he agreed. "This isn't the end, you know."

"It's not?" I asked.

"No. I'm not letting a girl like you get away that easily. I will be calling you."

"Good," I said, smiling.

"And who knows," he said, "maybe one day, I'll end up in Texas again. I just might have to take a trip to Farber to see the sights!"

"Oh, what sights there are to see!" I laughed.

"Yeah, well, you're there." Blue took both my hands into his and leaned in to kiss me. I closed my eyes to accept, but his kiss landed on my cheek. I smiled. "Goodnight, Laverne," he said. I actually liked hearing my name when he said it. It sounded so much nicer coming from him.

"Goodnight, Beauford," I said.

He took a few steps backward and waited for me to get inside my room before hopping back in the elevator. I sighed a happy sigh as I let myself fall back against the door. I then looked to the two empty beds in the room and remembered Leah upstairs with a drug addict rock star and a bag of cocaine. I scowled and screamed to myself angrily.

I tried to shake it off. Blue was right, Leah could take care of herself. She was a big girl, but I just couldn't stop worrying. I was really nervous for her. What was our relationship going to be like now? Everything may have just changed in one night with a stupid fight about money and one rendezvous with drugs and a lead singer. I felt betrayed and used. Not only was I out almost my entire school fund, but I was out one best friend. It didn't seem possible. It was a crazy nightmare I just couldn't wake from.

I lugged myself over to my suitcase and pulled out my pajamas. I took them into the bathroom with me and placed them next to the sink. I shut the bathroom door and started a hot shower. I thought that I could maybe wash away all the bad parts of the day. I stayed under the running water for about twenty minutes, letting it run down my body. The water felt great, but it didn't have any sort of miraculous healing effect. I still felt lousy about everything.

I got out, got dressed, brushed my teeth, combed my hair, and dragged myself out to choose a bed. When I got into the room, I noticed that one of the beds was already taken. Leah was under the covers, but I could tell she was still fully dressed, crying into one of the pillows.

"Leah?" I called out softly.

"I didn't do it, okay?" she shouted.

"You didn't do the drugs... or... Brick?" I asked carefully.

"Either one!"

"Okay, good." I was so relieved to hear that, but I was still angry with her for her awful behavior. Even so, I knew I should still be there for her if something was wrong. "You wanna talk about it?" I offered.

"I thought he wanted me, you know? Turns out, any female with a pulse will do," she sobbed. "You know he calls every girl angel? I guess it's just so he doesn't have to get any of their names straight. So gross."

"Well, I'm sorry, but I think it's for the best," I said, sitting down at the edge of her bed.

"God, L, I just wanted something great to happen, you know? I just wanted some great adventure I could feel good about. I wanted to be something."

HOW I SPENT MY SUMMER VACATION

"Well," I said, searching for the right thing to say, "I think we all want that, Leah, but after tonight, I don't think Brick Donovan and his little baggy are where it's at."

"Yeah, I know. I just, I don't know. I just feel so stupid." She looked up at me, her face a mess of snot and salty tears. I got up, grabbed her some tissue out of the bathroom, and came back to her.

"Here," I said, handing over the tissue.

"Thanks." She blew her nose into it a few times and then rubbed her face. "I'm so sorry, L. I've been horrible. I know I have. I'll get you the money."

"It's okay, Leah. We'll figure it out when we get home," I said.

"I just feel so terrible, about all of it, L. I'm really sorry," she apologized.

"I know, Leah. It's okay. I'm just glad you're okay. Wanna take a shower and watch some TV?" I asked.

"Yeah, okay." She got up and took herself into the bathroom.

I listened to the running water and mulled over the events of the night. I was really glad that Leah decided not to "party serious" with Brick. I was glad that she acknowledged what she had done to me.

While she was in the shower, I pulled out my phone and tried to figure out how many units I could still take in school with the money I had left over. After figuring books and supplies, it looked pretty bad. I would only be able to go super part time. I had enough for two classes and a gas tank home. Realistically, I still needed money for food, gas back and forth to school, and, I then realized, my next car payment and phone bill would soon be approaching. I hadn't exactly factored in the bills for the coming months. Before we left, I hadn't really thought ahead besides school tuition. I was in trouble. It didn't look good. In just a few short days, I had obliterated my school plan. I was so mad. I was mad, not just at Leah for being so frivolous with my money, but mostly I was now mad at myself for not knowing better and for not paying more attention to my own spending. How could I let things get so out of control?

The trip was over. We had no choice now but to go home. We didn't have the funds, nor the drive to continue. We no longer cared one bit about Brick Party Sundae, knowing what a mess they were as people, so the desire to follow them any longer had disappeared.

When Leah got back from her shower, I told her that I thought it was time we went home, and she agreed. We fell asleep to the glow of the television.

CHAPTER NINE

The morning came with a burst of light, which beamed persistently through the tiny space in the curtains. I got up and turned off the TV. I grappled with the idea of my morning call to my mother. I thought about telling her about my financial dilemma, as she was going to find out about it anyway, but I thought perhaps it would be best to have that horrible conversation face to face, and it might be even better if we had the discussion after I had first devised a plan to replenish my bank account.

After weighing my conversational options, I finally dialed my mom and simply told her that we'd decided to cut the trip short and were coming home. We'd seen all we needed to see and were burnt out. Unfortunately, because we weren't continuing on to our originally planned five additional destinations and looping around closer to home, the drive back was now over six long hours. It had to be done though, and we were ready.

We packed up our stuff quietly. We had made up enough to be cordial, but the tension was still there, and it was relatively uncomfortable. I was glad Leah had acknowledged her actions, but I still held her partially responsible for my current situation, and she knew it. Our usual bouncy, bubbly, laugh filled banter had been replaced with only necessary communication and long bouts of silence.

We checked out and gave our ticket to the valet guy for my car. He drove it around. As he pulled up to the entrance, I glanced over and noticed the Brick Party Sundae bus. No one was around it. It looked sad and alone. Instead of the excitement I had felt just the day before when seeing it, I felt disappointed and sickened. The car door opened and pulled my attention back to the task at hand, getting out of Millsberg as fast as possible. I tipped the valet guy, and he helped us load our things into the car.

Back on the road, things between us stayed pretty frozen. The first hour, aside from Leah telling me which highway we needed at the junction, we rode in silence. We didn't even turn on the radio. Finally, my stomach started growling so loudly, neither of us could ignore it. Leah laughed first, then me. My tummy was really noisy and really hungry.

"Wanna stop and get food?" I asked.

"Sure. My treat," she offered.

"Finally!" I joked. We both laughed.

We took an exit in a town called Glenville. There were several drive-thrus lined up along the main drag. We chose a familiar one. It was the same chain we always got our breakfast burritos at back in Farber.

Leah made good on her offer and got us both a breakfast burrito and a large coffee. We sat to enjoy our food.

"Take it off my tab," Leah joked, trying further to break the ice.

I laughed at her attempt, and we went on to make small conversation while we ate. She asked me about Blue, and I told her how sweet and gentlemanly he was and how he promised to call when he could. She made a few jokes about how amazing it was he turned out so great when his brother was such a loser. I could see she was still embarrassed about the night before.

"I guess I just have exceptionally bad taste in men," she said, laughing.

"Yes, you do," I joked. We laughed, and it almost felt comfortable, but there was still a feeling lingering over both of us that let us know that our relationship might never be quite the same again.

We took our coffees to the car and headed back out on the highway. We made some more small talk and finally turned the radio on. Of course, the very first song to come on was a hit by none other than Brick Party Sundae!

"Oh, eew!" Leah scoffed. "Turn it off! Turn it off!"

I grimaced at the dial as I flipped the station. We agreed to put in a CD instead, and Leah flipped through the book to find something other than BPS or Mel Says Go. We would eventually be able to listen to Mel Says Go again, but for the moment, their music was just a sore reminder of what we'd experienced in the presence of Brick Donovan.

She found a CD we could both enjoy, and she popped it in. We sang along to the tunes and danced around like we normally would as we headed on down the road. As soon as the disc ended, the silence crept up again. We really had nothing to talk about. Neither of us felt like playing the silly road games we'd played before. Leah had no choice but to fumble around for a new CD so that the awkward silence would end. She did this several times over throughout the trip home.

We stopped once at the four hour mark for gas, and we stopped a couple other times at rest stops for bathroom breaks. Each time, one of us would say something cute or small, the other would say something in response, and that was it. Other than that, there really wasn't any conversation between us, just music.

Though we were both bored and stuck in our own heads, Leah didn't dare fall asleep. I appreciated that. Even though we weren't talking to each other, it was nice to know that she was staying awake and alert for me while I drove. It was, I guess, her way of making an effort.

We finally arrived in Farber just before dinner time. I drove Leah up to her house, and I got out to help her unload her things.

"Well," I said, "I guess now that we're back early, your mom will never know that we didn't go camping."

"Yeah." She laughed. "I think I might come clean about that. We'll see."

"Well, good luck," I said, closing my trunk.

"Thanks." She picked up her bags and turned to go into her house. She paused and turned back toward me. "L," she said, "we're okay, right?"

I thought for a second. We weren't really okay. Things between us might never be okay. I wasn't really sure what the answer was.

"We'll get there," I said plainly and smiled a short smile. Maybe we would. I couldn't say for sure at that moment.

"Okay." She turned back toward her house and walked away.

I watched her walk up the walkway and into her house. Becca came to the window and waved at me. I waved back and smiled at her. I let out a huge breath. My stomach turned. It hit me that I would now have to go home and tell my parents what had happened and that I didn't have enough money for tuition. They would be insanely furious. All they ever wanted for me was to find my path in life, and I had assured them that I would find it in college. How could I tell them that college was now impossible? Knowing them, they would likely pitch in the tuition just to get me to go, but it would cost me in the long run. It would cost my pride and their faith in me. They would be so disappointed to know that I blew through my future. Sure, it would eventually die down, and things would go back to normal, but the initial sting was going to be pretty painful.

Then a brilliant yet horrible idea came to me. Marnie. There were still ten days before early enrollment, so I could sign up for a couple classes then, and then, during regular enrollment, if I had the money, I could try to get the rest of my classes. If I could get my job back, I could make the two hundred I needed for the units, and my parents might only have to help me a tiny bit with books. It was a plan I feared. It was something I didn't want to do, but I realized, that's life. I guess that's what being a grown up is all about. Being responsible means that you have to do things you might not want to do; you have to just suck it up and do them for the greater good. I doubt my parents wanted to work as hard as they had all these years, but they did it. They did it for us, for me. I had to do this.

I brushed my hair out and used my purse makeup kit to freshen up my face. I took a few long, deep breaths, started my car, and headed over to Miss Marnie's to grovel and beg for my job back.

I walked into the place, expecting to find Ben or maybe even a new hire, but Marnie was actually there. I was sort of taken aback to see her in an apron, holding a bar mop. As I approached her, she looked at me with disdain. She greeted me with equal distaste.

"What are you doing here?" she asked coldly.

"I came to apologize. I'm so sorry I left like that. It was childish and irresponsible, and I am so sorry," I said, trying to sound as sincere as possible.

"You didn't even tell me you were quitting. You just walked out and left poor Ben here to fend for himself," she reminded.

"Yes, poor Ben," I said, biting my tongue. Ben wasn't a poor anything, but I had to play this cool.

"I tried calling you, you know. You didn't answer. We were worried about you. That is until I called your house, and your mother told me you were off touring the country to see some band." Marnie's lips pursed and her forehead crinkled.

"I know. I'm so sorry. It was stupid, but I'm back, and I was really hoping..."

"Oh, you want your job back?" she asked, cutting me short.

"Yes, very much so. I like it here," I lied.

"Well, given the circumstance of your leaving I should turn you away and never let you set foot in here again, but being the civilized, forgiving person I am, I might be willing to give you a second chance, provided you can start tomorrow, and you're willing to work a double."

"Yes! Sure! Thank you!" I shouted gleefully. She obviously hadn't found anyone to replace me or Stacey, so the timing couldn't have been better. I counted myself lucky that this worked out the way it did. I may not have been a fan of working there, but the news of a double shift was the most exciting thing I'd heard all day. I could build up that school fund in no time.

"Whatever. Get out of here. Be back tomorrow at seven a.m. sharp! You're opening." She waved her hand at me to leave.

"Thank you! Thank you!" I yelled excitedly as I ran out the door. This was fantastic. This would definitely help when I told my parents about the monetary mess I'd worked myself into.

I drove home, happy as could be. I had a purpose. I had a direction. I was going to work in the morning, and I was going to start school with everybody else; everybody except Leah. My face sunk as I remembered that Leah wouldn't be beside me when I registered. She wouldn't be in all the same classes, or even on the campus. We wouldn't be sharing lunch together in the common, and we wouldn't be dishing about our teachers and fellow classmates. I was on my own.

I pulled up to my house and parked, dreading the walk inside. When I opened the front door, I could smell something cooking. It smelled fantastic. My mom had made her famous spaghetti and meatballs. Knowing that she had made one of my favorite dinners only made me feel worse.

"Hey, welcome home, traveler!" My dad greeted as I

walked into the living room.

"Hi, Dad." I said happily, trying to mask my debt guilt.

"So, you girls decided to pack it in early, huh? What happened, LL Cool J? You run out of money?" He laughed. If only he knew, he wouldn't have been laughing.

"Actually, yeah, something like that," I admitted.

"What?" He wasn't laughing anymore.

"I kind of need to talk to you guys."

My dad called out for my mom to come in from the kitchen. Luckily, she had just finished cooking, so she had some time to sit without the threat of burning something. I told them all about our budget and our "plan." I told them that, while I should have kept a better eye on the spending myself, it wasn't entirely my own doing. I spilled about Leah and how she had basically used me and pretty much ruined the entire trip. My parents were angry but somewhat sympathetic. According to them, I should have known better than to let someone else control my wallet. They were right about that. I learned that lesson for sure.

They weren't too happy to hear about my run ins with the band either. Yes, that's right, I told them all about our time spent with the amazing let down that is Brick Party Sundae and how it added to my decision to come home. They agreed that I did the right thing calling off the second half of the journey, and they were happy to hear that I had a plan to go back to work and make up the money I'd blown for tuition. After all was laid out, they told me they would help me out if I needed it. I was relieved that they were so cool and calm about everything. They were disappointed, and who could blame them? But it did go a lot smoother than I had played it in my head. I'm pretty sure the manning up and crawling back to Miss Marnie's was my saving grace in this whole situation. I'm glad I made that choice.

Once we got it all out in the open, I felt a whole lot better. My parents didn't yell or reprimand the way I thought they might, and we got to enjoy Mom's homemade meatballs without the gloom of a heavy argument hanging over us. It was good to be home.

After dinner, I went to my room and flipped on the light. I sighed a deep, sad sigh as I looked around and saw the multiple Brick Donovans staring back at me. I was so tired from the day, but I had to get rid of them. They had to go right that instant. As I pulled out the pins and tore each photo, cutout, and poster from the wall, I felt a sort of peace wash over me. I felt like this was a new beginning, maybe a new me, a slightly more mature and evolved version of me anyway. I mulled over the various disappointments of the trip as I ripped away at the images. I didn't feel jaded or angry anymore; instead, I felt older and a little more in tune with what the world is really like. The pure white broke through and illuminated my room in a new way. I balled up the waste into a pile on the floor and stepped back to look at my new, clean beginning. The walls were nearly bare, and it felt great. I took the mess to the outside trash and then got ready for bed. That night, I slept a deep, comfortable sleep. It was dreamless; it was perfect.

CHAPTER TEN

The next morning, I found myself back at Miss Marnie's, greeting customers and serving pancake platters. It was the same job I loathed just a couple weeks before, but it was somehow a much happier place to be. I guess it was because, this time around, I appreciated that what I was doing at this horrible place was going to take me somewhere better. It seemed worth it, and that kept a smile on my face the whole day.

The next week was pretty much life as usual, minus the presence of Leah. I hadn't seen or heard from her since I dropped her off upon our return from the road trip from Hell. I was a little disappointed that she hadn't tried to contact me but not at all surprised. I hadn't exactly been wearing out my thumbs trying to text or call her either, so I guess the lull was mutual. I missed her, but I didn't know if I was ready to really be around her just yet.

By the following Monday, I had earned enough in tips to afford one more class, so I visited the MFCC campus for early enrollment. I was able to at least get the three classes I wanted most. Final enrollment was only a week away, and classes started just a couple days after that, so I knew I might not get the final two courses I wanted. While I was there, I grabbed an extra course schedule. I took it to work with me so that I could look over my options during the slow periods.

I got to work that afternoon to find a super smiley Ben on the shift before mine.

"Hey there, college girl!" he said.

"Hey there, college dropout," I said, joking... kind of.

"Hey!" he snorted. "I'm not a dropout. I never enrolled in the first place. There's a difference. Besides I have the restaurant biz going for me."

"Oh, okay then. Good for you." I laughed. "Glad you have it worked out."

"So, I haven't seen your hot little friend around lately. What's she up to?"

"First, eew. Second, I have no idea." I frowned.

"Aw, what? Did you two break up?" He made a falsely empathetic pout and laughed at me. "Whatever. You'll get over it. You just need to make new friends so I have something nice to look at when you're here."

"Uh, again eew, and gee thanks." I stuck my tongue out at him, and he disappeared around the back with a cigarette hanging loosely from his trout-like mouth.

I tied my apron strings behind me and looked around. The tables were empty. I figured I had a few minutes before Benny Boy came back, so I pulled out the course catalog I had swiped from the campus earlier.

As I flipped past my top choices and thumbed through the alternatives, I heard a familiar jangle at the front door. I quickly folded the booklet and threw it under the register.

"Hey, it's just me," a voice said. It was Leah's voice. I looked up to see Leah standing in front of the register with one hand in her pocket and an envelope in the other hand.

"Oh," I said, "hi." I looked down for a second, searching for something to say but not finding it. I looked back to her blankly.

"I just..." She was having a hard time finding her words too. "I just... well... here." She handed me the envelope.

I took it in my hand. "What's this?" I asked.

"It's the money I owe you. Well, some of it anyway. I'm like eighty bucks shy, but I'll get it to you."

I flipped back the top of the envelope to reveal a mishmash of denominations. I didn't count it; I was sure it was there, minus the eighty like she'd said.

"Thanks. How did you..."

"Oh, I decided to start putting my talents to use," she said, smiling.

I shot her a sarcastic sideways glance.

"No! Not that!" She shouted, laughing. "I thought I'd give the scalping thing a try, just more legit. I put some crap up online for auction, and I hawked my Brick Donovan autograph. I mean, he owes us, right? I figured I might as well make some money off the suck weasel."

I laughed at the idea that Brick owed us for being such a jerk. "Makes sense. Thank you."

"Sure. Fair's fair." She moved toward me one step, hesitated, and leaned back, folding her arms.

There was a semi awkward pause. I was suddenly very aware of the ticking of the clock behind me. It became uncomfortably loud as we just stood there.

"So," she said, finally cutting the silence. "You maybe wanna hang out sometime or something?"

"Yeah," I said, not hesitating. I really did. I missed her a lot. I missed the Leah I knew anyway. I was hoping that the old Leah I knew and loved was the Leah that I was talking to now and not the one I went on the nightmare tour with.

"Cool. So, I'll call you?" She smiled.

"Cool."

She turned to leave but then turned and came forward a few steps.

"You were right, you know," she said.

"About what?" I cocked my head.

"Pretty much everything. I *am* sorry, like really sorry."

"I know." I knew she was being sincere. Leah was back.

"Oh, and my mom said she'd help out with school, so I

will be enrolling, just not for full time. I've kind of got a debt to settle," she said, laughing. "But, no, seriously, I'll be taking a couple classes. I'm going over now for the early enrollment thingy. You go yet?"

"Yeah, I went before I came in," I said. I was really excited to hear that Leah was going to be coming to school. I wanted to jump up and down and do the L Squared secret handshake with her, but I didn't. I was, however, hopeful that we might be on our way to mending our broken relationship, so I walked over to my purse and got her the course list I'd just signed up for. "If you can get any of these three, you'll have a friendly face sitting next to you," I said, handing her the sheet and a blank guest check and pen to copy it down with.

"Cool. Thanks, L. I'll try." She smiled wide and copied the info onto the ticket. "So, call you later?"

"Sure."

"Alright," she said as she turned to leave again. "Bye!"

"Bye!"

And she was back out the door, leaving the jingle jangle of the bells to fill the entry way.

I looked over the list in my hand. There were three general education requirements staring back at me. I wasn't looking forward to them, but I knew I had to get them out of the way. I was, however, curious as to my other options for the two classes I had yet to sign up for. I didn't necessarily have to stick to the gen-ed list. I looked through the booklet. Some of the more exciting courses had a laundry list of prerequisites, so they were out of the question for the time being. Then something stood out. Creative Writing. It only required that I at least be enrolled in English 101, which I already was. I had always been interested in writing; I'd just never taken it or myself very seriously before. Maybe it was time I gave it a real shot. As I tossed the idea around in my head, the door jingled it's annoying tune again, and a customer appeared in the entry way.

"Hi," I greeted, grabbing a menu. "One?"

The last days of summer came and went with no particular excitement to speak of. Greg texted me at one point. He sent a three part text about how sorry he was. Apparently single life wasn't as fruitful as he had hoped it would be, and he wanted to work things out. I didn't text him back.

I talked quite frequently with Blue, who was wrapping up the tour and excited to get home. He said that he had enrolled himself in classes online and would be starting school soon too. He told Brick that he wanted to leave the band and life on the road once the tour ended, and I guess it caused a big blow up, but they made up, and Brick was already on to the next distraction. Blue said Brick wouldn't have any trouble finding a new road manager, though he might have trouble keeping one.

Blue and I made a pact to stay in touch and see each other during winter break. We didn't work out the details, but he said he'd fly to Texas if he had to. I think we'll make it work.

Leah and I have been texting and talking as well. We still haven't really hung out since we got back from our little excursion, but she did get one of the same classes, so we'll be spending more time together soon. She says she'll get me the rest of the money by the end of next month, but it doesn't really seem all that important anymore. It was never really about the money so much as it was about the stranger she'd become in just a few short days. She seems to be back to her usual self now, whatever that is. L Squared won't be buying team t-shirts anytime soon, but we're working on it.

I made it to the final registration and was actually able to get the last two classes I wanted for the semester. I decided to take Creative Writing after all. Maybe one day I'll be a big writer like those people who write those vampire and werewolf books. I can write these beautiful, dreamlike novels, and Blue can do the cover art. I know. I know. I'm getting way ahead of myself, but a girl can dream.

So here I am today. I just completed my very first day as a college student, and I have to say, it wasn't so bad. The teachers of course called me Laverne during roll call, but no one snickered, and I actually didn't mind the sound of it. I like the campus, I know a few people in each class, and Leah will be in the math class I start tomorrow. I love love love my Creative Writing teacher, Mr. Falk. He's a trip.

Today's class was so much fun. We barely got settled in, and first thing, he assigned us this writing exercise.

"So here's what we're going to do," Mr. Falk said, "we're, and by *we're*, I mean *you're*, because I won't be writing anything..." Funny, right? He went on, "We're going to be writing a little something that may seem sort of familiar, and a lot of you might think it's lame, but I like to do this because it gives me a sense of your writing style and of who I'm going to be up here talking to every day."

Now at this point, I was getting incredibly nervous. He wanted to know my writing style? Do I have one of those? What does that even mean? Was he asking if I use cursive or print? I didn't know what he was talking about.

So he said, "the title of your piece will be *How I Spent My Summer Vacation.*"

I was thinking, *is he for real*? I'm pretty sure I remember writing these what I did last summer essays in like second and third grade.

"So you're all probably thinking, is this guy for real? I wrote that in like second grade." Yes, he actually said that after I thought it. Weird. "The answer is," he went on, "yes! I am for real. It will be fun. What I want from you is whatever you want to give me. You can write a summary about your entire summer. You can make up a poem about your days spent by the pool. You can write a story in third person about one particular event that you most enjoyed or most hated from your summer experience; it's up to you. Make it fun. Make it you. You have twenty minutes. And... go!"

And so we started. I glanced around. Some of the students were scrolling away as fast as they could, others were sitting there, pen in mouth, staring blankly at their note paper, and a couple others, like me, were looking around to see what everyone else was doing. I opened my college ruled notebook and pulled the cap off my brand new plastic pen. I looked at the carefully printed lines on the page and wrote out my title: *How I Spent My Summer Vacation.*

As I stared at the title, a wave of memories came over me. I remembered Greg and how he dumped me like a brick. I remembered the nights I wasted crying over it and the days I spent wishing things were different. I reflected on my job, quitting, and then going back on hands and knees. I thought about Leah and how excited she was to tell me all about her crazy plan to follow Brick Party Sundae around Texas. I smiled, remembering her exuberance. I thought back to the fights we had and how disappointed we were when we found out that Brick was human and not some super golden demigod. Then I thought about Blue and how perfect and charming and wonderful he is. Of all the things we went through over the summer, I did manage to get him out of it. Even if we can't find a way to make it work, my memories of how I felt being with him those few days will always be happy ones. And then, a burst of inspiration came to me, and my hand started moving back and forth over the paper. I was writing. I was creating. I was telling a story; an amazing story. It was the story of my crazy, band chasing, trouble making, money losing, lesson learning, self-discovering summer.

Thinking back on all of it now, I wouldn't change a thing. I learned so much about life and about human nature and about myself. I'm glad we went, because now, for the first time maybe ever, I have some direction. I've seen things outside of Farber, and I know I want to make a real life for myself. I want it to be interesting and fun and meaningful, and I'm excited to see where the road takes me.

No matter what comes at me, and no matter what joys and disasters I come across along the way, I will never, ever forget how I spent my summer vacation.

NOTE FROM THE AUTHOR

Thank you for reading *How I Spent My Summer Vacation*. I hope you enjoyed it. I had a lot of fun creating L Squared and their crazy adventures. While this entire story is fabricated, I had my own share of misadventures growing up. A lot of the things portrayed in this book are dangerous, and let's face it, illegal; that said, I do not recommend testing these particular boundaries yourself. But, life does happen. Growing is learning. Be safe, be kind, and just be you.

Remember to always dream big and follow your heart. All things are possible with imagination and determination.

-Elizabeth Fields

elizabethfields.net

Made in the USA
Charleston, SC
26 May 2012